Strange Invaders

Suddenly Cheeky gave a soft *yeeep* of warning. Blade looked up and saw that he and the feather-monkey were no longer alone.

A number of dark-skinned men were climbing down the slope on the far bank of the river, moving sure-footedly from the cover of one boulder to another. They were closing in on both sides of the mouth of a canyon that opened on the riverbank. The canyon's floor was level but it twisted so sharply that Blade could see barely fifty yards into it. From somewhere up the canyon a cloud of dust rose.

Blade counted at least twenty men. Fortunately all their attention seemed to be on the mouth of the canyon. Blade's camouflage coveralls were also doing a good job of hiding him against the dark gravel of the riverbank. He easily found cover for himself and Cheeky before the men reached the bank of the river.

The men's skins were brown with a tinge of bronze, and their hair long, dark, and glossy. Most of them wore nothing but sandals and leather loinguards; some were completely naked. The ones with loinguards seemed to have daggers thrust into their belts; all carried spears with wicked-looking barbed heads and tufts of feathers at the butt ends. Some had their hair tied up with vividly colored headbands. More than anything else, they made Blade think of a hunting party of North American Indians before the white man came.

BLADE

WARRIORS OF LATAN
Jeffrey Lord

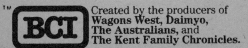

™ **BCI** Created by the producers of
**Wagons West, Daimyo,
The Australians,** and
The Kent Family Chronicles.

Chairman of the Board: Lyle Kenyon Engel

PINNACLE BOOKS NEW YORK

BLADE #37: WARRIORS OF LATAN

Copyright © 1984 by Book Creations, Inc.

An original Pinnacle Books edition, published for the first time anywhere.

First printing/April 1984

ISBN: 0-523-41211-8

Can. ISBN: 0-523-43229-1

Cover illustration by Kevin Johnson

Printed in the United States of America

PINNACLE BOOKS, INC.
1430 Broadway
New York, New York 10018

9 8 7 6 5 4 3 2 1

WARRIORS OF LATAN

Chapter 1

"Halloooo, Richard!"

The ballroom of the old country house was large enough to raise echoes. Lord Leighton's voice, J thought, might be powerful enough to raise ghosts, if the old place had any left. The scientist was past eighty, hunchbacked; his legs were twisted by polio, and he walked with the aid of a cane. He still had a powerful voice, however—not to mention a sharp tongue, which J had felt more than a few times.

The two men heard thumpings and footsteps from somewhere above, then a shrill *yeeep-yeeep-yeeep* that grew rapidly louder. "He's home," said Leighton.

The scientist appeared to be bracing himself, with his knob-knuckled hands gripping his cane tightly. Lately he had taken to using a cane outside his laboratories. Possibly he really needed it, but J suspected it also contained a few disagreeable surprises for any would-be kidnapper or assassin. Tear gas, poison darts, a miniature hand grenade? J wasn't going to ask merely to satisfy his curiosity; as long as he didn't know anything official about the cane, he wouldn't have to answer the questions of nervous civilian authorities.

A loaded cane made excellent sense if Leighton was going to be moving about very much in the world outside his laboratories. The mind inside that bald head had been

1

one of the great scientific talents of modern England for half a century. Now it held the most vital secret of all— the secret of Dimension X. And it was the responsibility of J, as head of security and intelligence, to keep that secret safe, to keep the mission functioning smoothly, preventing the interference of Russians, Chinese, or anyone else who would want to explore the unknown.

Before J could follow that line of thought any further, something small shot out of a hole in the ceiling like a missile. It seemed to have homing properties as it shot across the ceiling toward J, then dropped down on his shoulder.

"Hello, Cheeky," J said.

The missile was a monkeylike creature, about two feet from its head to the base of a long tail. In place of fur, however, Cheeky had glossy blue feathers. In the dusty and decayed grandeur of the old house, he was an exotic splash of color.

He started pulling J's hair with one paw while he ran the other through his feathers, combing out dust and bits of plaster. J knew the hair-pulling was a gesture of affection, but still didn't want to wind up as bald as a tomato because the feather-monkey liked him so much.

Footsteps sounded behind the two men, and they turned to see Richard Blade striding toward them. No matter how tired or work-stained or casually dressed he was, Richard always strode, never just walked, unless he was too badly hurt to be on his feet at all. Standing six feet one, he moved his two hundred and ten pounds of muscle and bone with the deceptively easy grace of a tiger on the prowl—a grace that hid more than a tiger's deadliness.

Of course, if Richard Blade hadn't been as lethal as he was, he almost certainly would have been dead a long time ago, far away. Richard Blade was the other half of the secret of Dimension X—the only man whose qualities of mind and body let him travel time after time into a series of deadly and bizarre parallel worlds, the only living human being who could travel into Dimension X and return alive and sane.

Dimension X was discovered quite by accident, like so much else in the history of science. Lord Leighton was experimenting with hooking up Richard Blade's brain to what was then his most advanced computer, hoping to create a superior combination of human and electronic intelligence. Leighton had hoped Blade's superior mental and physical abilities would be enhanced by connecting him to a computer, and that Blade would, in turn, improve the computers capabilities. Direct interaction, it was called, but instead of learning all the information stored in the computer, Blade was hurled off into the unknown, from which he returned only by the use of his wits and strength, with a good deal of luck thrown in.

Obviously the ability to explore a parallel Dimension, with lands that mirrored Home Dimension, and use their resources would be enormously valuable to England. So Project Dimension X was born.

A few years and a few million pounds later, they'd actually made some progress—although not much in proportion to the time and money spent, not to mention the number of scars on various portions of Richard Blade's anatomy.

As he always did, seeing Blade again after an interval, J studied the younger man closely. He didn't expect to see any changes, and didn't. Blade was older, wiser, and more experienced than he'd been when they first met. J was head of the secret military intelligence agency MI6A then, and Blade was its newest field agent, straight out of Oxford. Today Blade still walked alone, a man born into the wrong century, better fit for the life of a professional adventurer than anyone else J had ever met.

As Blade appeared, Cheeky let out a wild *yeeeep* of delight and launched himself from J's shoulder toward his master and friend. He forgot to let go of J's hair as he did, and a large tuft of it went with the feather-monkey. J winced and rubbed the spot.

"Cheeky, that was *bad* of you," said Blade sharply, lightly slapping the feather-monkey about the head and shoulders several times.

"*Mreeeep?*" said Cheeky. He sounded contrite, but it was hard to tell what he was thinking. The only person who could was Blade himself. He'd found Cheeky in Dimension X, among the warring lords of the Crimson River, and immediately established a telepathic link with the feather-monkey. The two could communicate by sending each other mental images or pictures. Their minds seemed to communicate without the use of their senses, and this strange bond tied them together in a close relationship that Blade had never known with any human.

That telepathic link, J now knew, might be one of the biggest advances the Project ever made. Or at least that was Leighton's best guess—not that he was ever willing to admit that he was "guessing," of course. He regarded "guessing" as an obscene act. Nevertheless, the peculiar bond between Cheeky and Blade seemed to enable the feather-monkey to travel into other Dimensions, too. Maybe now the scientists were close to discovering how to send other human beings to Dimension X.

With a subdued Cheeky on his shoulder, Blade led the way to the part of the house that he had already cleaned and redecorated. He had bought the country house for himself a short time ago; it was to be his haven in Home Dimension, a place to house the growing menagerie of creatures he brought back with him from his strange travels. Built in the eighteenth century and neglected since before the Second World War, the house was going to need even more work before it was really comfortable. But at least you could move about through it now without falling through the floors or having portions of the ceiling fall on *you*.

Blade removed dustcovers from three chairs and pointed

to a fine mahogany sideboard on top of which were glasses, bottles of liquor, and a dish of dried fruits and nuts. "If you gentlemen can make free with the contents of the sideboard, I'll go take a shower. Cheeky will play host."

"*Yeeeeekkkkkkhhhhh!*"

J looked at Blade. "You almost said that with a straight face."

"Who? Me or Cheeky?"

"You."

"Too bad. I didn't mean it as a joke." Blade set Cheeky on the floor and went out. The two men stared at Cheeky, then at each other.

"If I thought Richard was playing a practical joke—" began Leighton indignantly.

J waved a hand in dismissal of that idea. "He's about the last man in the world to do that. No, I think he really does expect us to treat Cheeky as our host." J went over to the sideboard and poured out two glasses of scotch for himself and Leighton and handed the mixed fruits and nuts to Cheeky. The feather-monkey picked up the dish, *yeeeeped* something that might have been "Thank you," and then jumped up on top of the sideboard without spilling a thing from the dish and started nibbling.

Leighton was silent as he took his glass, then shook his head again. "If Richard isn't joking, what does he think Cheeky is?"

"Or *who*. Remember, he always calls Cheeky 'he.' "

"I'm not likely to forget it."

"Oh, confound it, Leighton! Why don't you stop beating around the bush and come out and say that you think Richard's gone bonkers! You're thinking it so loudly *I* can hear you, and I'm not telepathic."

Leighton drained his glass and set it firmly on a closed container of plastering compound, then made a steeple of his long fingers. "I'm not worried about Blade's sanity, J. I hope you realize that if I were, I would have said so."

J nodded. Leighton wasn't as close to Richard as he

was. J had known Richard longer and better, seeing him almost as the son he never had. Leighton, in contrast, had started off seeing Richard as hardly better than some exotic and expensive sort of laboratory animal. He'd mellowed over time, though—it was only a rumor that he had a computer where his heart should be.

"What bothers me is something else," Leighton went on. "Suppose this bond between Richard and Cheeky gets so close that it's impossible for Richard to link telepathically with anyone else we might want to send to Dimension X?"

"If there *is* anyone else."

"Now who's being skeptical about telepathy?" said Leighton, with a twinkle in his eye. "Oh, I admit I was one of those who dismissed it. So damned many charlatans running around, it was hardly worthwhile picking out the real phenomena. But I can face facts. Richard's not a superman, not a mutant, not some creature from outer space. He's as human as you and I. Where there's one like him, there have to be others."

"First catch your rabbit," quoted J.

"Precisely. Unfortunately, because of all those bloody charlatans, we'll have to devise our own methods of finding telepaths."

"And I suppose for that you'll be asking the Prime Minister for another hundred thousand pounds from the Special Fund?"

"I suppose so," said Leighton bluntly. "Of course, the Russians have done a significant amount of real research into the paranormal. I'm certain my contacts there would give me a substantial—" He stopped as he heard the spymaster starting to choke at the idea of asking the Russians for help.

After a bit, J calmed down and took another swallow of whiskey. He really *ought* to stop rising to Leighton's baits that way! He sipped more whiskey and considered other possibilities raised by Blade's telepathic ability with

Cheeky. For instance, suppose the bond between Blade and Cheeky grew so close that Blade ceased to be interested in forming relationships with those who didn't have telepathic abilities. Could Blade even lose interest in women? That could be dismissed as a fantasy. Richard would probably flirt with the nurse watching over his deathbed!

Or suppose Richard got so used to the link with Cheeky that he came to want the same link with a woman? Did that mean their elusive telepath, whom they hoped to send to Dimension X when Blade could no longer perform, would have to be a woman? And what if the woman was too badly needed for traveling into Dimension X to stay close to Blade . . . ? Sooner or later, Blade would no longer be fast enough and tough enough to survive easily in Dimension X, and he would have to be replaced. When that happened, Blade's life work would be over. If there wasn't anyone waiting to help him make a new life . . .

Things could get a trifle complicated in that event, J realized. He tried to sort out the possibilities, conscious as he was of a distaste for speculating on Richard's personal life in this manner. Richard was, after all, a grown man.

Before J could take this line of thought much further, he was interrupted by the return of a freshly showered Blade. The younger man poured himself a strong whiskey and sat down, then fixed the other with a wry look.

"Well, what grand plans and schemes do you have for your guinea pigs this time?"

"Actually, Richard—nothing," said Leighton. "Or at least nothing except trying to land both you and Cheeky in the same place this time!"

"I should bloody well hope so!" exclaimed Blade, and Cheeky made emphatic noises of agreement. They both remembered all too well their separation during the transition to Kaldak, when they landed in separate places in the

Dimension. "What do you want us to do to help matters?"

"I think the telepathy is the key to getting you and Cheeky or you and anybody else to land together," said Leighton. "If you and Cheeky can concentrate on holding mental contact right through the transition, that will give you a better chance."

"You're assuming the new booth is sufficiently fool-proof so that I don't need to be alert for its playing tricks?"

"Yes."

Blade nodded slowly. "That's reasonable enough. In fact, even if it did have some bugs left in it, there's not much I could do about them during the actual transition. Much better to concentrate on staying with Cheeky. Right, little friend?" He scratched the feather-monkey, who *yeeeped* in agreement. "Is there anything we should do besides concentrate?"

"I sincerely wish I could suggest something, Richard," said Leighton. He summarized his conversation with J. "I suspect that the most reliable method we've ever had available for telepathy is Cheeky himself. Unfortunately, there's only one of him."

"I could leave him behind—" began Blade, but Cheeky interrupted him, squeaking angrily and making faces at everybody. Obviously he was determined to stay with Blade, sink or swim.

"Your friend doesn't seem to care for the idea," said Leighton dryly. "If we don't send him through this time, we won't be able to field-test the telepathic link. I also suspect that the first few times we use Cheeky to test for telepathy, we'll need you around to communicate with him. I do appreciate your willingness to leave him in our hands, but it's not necessary this time."

Leighton looked meditatively at the cracked plaster of the ceiling while he sipped more of his drink. "Actually, there is one more thing you could do. Would you object to reducing the amount of equipment you take with you? Or at least the amount of metal?''

J started to protest. One of the great blessings of the new booth was that it created an electrical field that flowed evenly around Blade, undisturbed by anything he wore or carried. This allowed him to go into Dimension X properly equipped for both battle and survival. "Why metal?" asked J. "*Is* there something wrong with the electrical field after all?"

"No. It's the telepathy I'm thinking about. Suppose it was all the metal in Richard's gear that disturbed the link last time?"

J didn't disagree. At least it was a comparatively reasonable hypothesis. However, he couldn't resist a chance to twit the scientist. "That sounds rather like the old legends about the fairy folk who were vulnerable to cold iron. What have you been reading lately?"

Leighton started to glare, then chuckled when he realized that J was pulling his leg. "If one assumes that paranormal powers exist, and that the 'fairy folk' were a people who had them—well, the legends make a certain amount of sense. Or at least as much sense as anything else in this whole confounded business!"

"No doubt," said J. "And also, if we can equip Richard adequately, so that what he takes with him will help him to survive but won't look too peculiar to the people of another Dimension, it will help protect the Dimension X secret."

Blade choked on his drink and muttered something that sounded to J rather like "Bugger the Dimension X secret." J almost sympathized with the sentiment. Richard had been through a good deal on his return to the Dimension of Kaldak to protect the Dimension X secret. The Kaldakans had looked upon him suspiciously because of the strange equipment he carried, and in order to avoid interrogation about how he had come to be in Kaldak, he had to go to great pains, including nearly committing incest with his own daughter.

"I dislike admitting this," said Leighton slowly, "but I find myself compelled to suggest that perhaps there is no such thing as the Dimension X secret." Both J and Blade stared at him.

"Consider the Wizard of Rentoro, who traveled into Dimension X by his own unaided mental powers," Leighton continued. "Consider the Menel, the space-traveling aliens who seem to exist in more than one Dimension. Consider how little we know for certain about Dimension X and how to get from here to there. Then ask yourself—*are* we the only people who know about Dimension X? I find it increasingly difficult to be terribly optimistic on that point."

With the proposition stated that way, J found it hard not to agree with the scientist. "If that's the case, we'll have to be particularly careful about security for our research in telepathy. Computers like ours don't exactly grow on hedges, but almost anybody with a thousand pounds' worth of laboratory and equipment can study the paranormal.

"We may not have the only path between the Dimensions. But I'd wager we have the most reliable one. I still want to make sure that everybody else who develops an equally reliable one is on our side."

They could all drink to that.

Chapter 2

One moment Blade and Cheeky were surrounded by the wire-mesh booth that was linked up to the computer in the Project laboratory. The next moment there was nothing except the indescribable *otherness* between the Dimensions. Blade lost awareness of his body, and he couldn't tell that he was gritting his teeth and clenching his fists in an effort to hole the mental link with Cheeky so they could land in Dimension X side by side.

The sense of the *otherness* around him grew stronger, but the sense of Cheeky's mind linked to his grew no weaker. Blade let himself hope for the best. He also began to expect one of the psychedelic displays he'd endured in transitions using the old booth with its electrodes, before the KALI capsule and all the changes since then.

Before that happened, there was a sudden *pop* of changing air pressure, so sudden that Blade had to swallow to clear his ears. He felt chilly breezes on his face, and underfoot a sloping surface of loose stones.

Then the stones started to slide, and he started to slide with them. He shouted a warning to Cheeky both with his mind and with his voice and threw himself backward, arms outflung to either side. His head struck the rocks with jarring force, but the downward slide stopped. The rattle and clunk of the sliding stones came to an abrupt end. An unpleasantly long time later, he heard the faint sound of

11

those stones hitting the bottom of something a long way down.

All this happened so fast that Blade hadn't opened his eyes while his trained reflexes were operating. Now he looked up to see cold blue sky overhead, and Cheeky's small face peering worriedly into his own. Since Cheeky's face was completely covered with feathers, it was rather hard to read his expressions. However, the mental message was clear—a picture of Cheeky sitting and mourning by Blade's corpse, with an implied question added. As clearly as if he'd been speaking English, Cheeky was asking, *Are you all right*?"

Blade sent a mental picture of himself running around in circles and beating his chest like Tarzan, the picture of health. Cheeky made relieved noises. Then Blade opened the mouth of the nylon carrying bag that held Cheeky snugly on his chest. The feather-monkey scrambled out, jumped up and down to stretch his limbs, then scrambled up the slope to level ground, squeaking in protest as sharp stones bruised his paws. Blade followed Cheeky on hands and knees until he was sure of his footing, then rushed the rest of the distance.

Blade's rush sent more stones rattling down the slope to vanish into space. The slope lay on the edge of a canyon, the floor of which was about a mile wide, with a river running through it. In some places the wall of the canyon was climbable, but where Blade had landed it was more than a hundred feet straight down. If he and Cheeky had gone over the edge . . .

Leighton and his researchers might someday solve all the problems of reaching Dimension X, but they still wouldn't solve most of the problems of staying alive once you got there. Blade hoped anyone who went with him in the future would know that, or at least learn it fast. Otherwise the search for a new Dimension X traveler might have to start all over again right away.

The scenery was spectacular but monotonous—

alternating stretches of rock, gray-brown hills, and dense blue forest. On the horizon he could make out high mountains, their lower slopes wrapped in more forest and their peaks white with snow.

Blade decided to follow the canyon down to the river, then follow the river wherever it led him. Rivers usually led to human beings sooner or later, with fish to eat and water to drink on the way. He turned left, heading for the nearest place where the side of the canyon looked climbable.

The movement dislodged more stones, and Blade climbed a little farther away from the edge before going on. Cheeky made approving noises, and sent a picture of Blade lying a bloody and twisted corpse among the boulders at the bottom of the canyon.

A moment later, Cheeky's squeals and the rattle of falling stones were drowned out by a deep rumbling growl from the depths of the canyon. Before the echoes of the first growl died, another one came, and a whole chorus after that. Other cries followed, sounding more like steam whistles than anything made by a living throat. Blade and Cheeky both drew their knives and stepped back a few more yards from the canyon.

Gradually the growls and cries died away. Blade listened carefully and sniffed the air. For the first time he noticed a faint miasma floating up from the canyon—the unmistakable odor of large quantities of well-rotted meat.

Something—several somethings—had their lair down in the canyon. They were large, they were carnivorous, and they sounded hungry, angry, or maybe both. Blade decided to stay out of the canyon. He didn't want anything able to make a noise like that behind him while he was scrambling over boulders that would keep him from moving fast.

Before he started off again, Blade unslung the light rucksack from his back and pulled out a cloth-wrapped bundle. A few minutes' work, and a tangle of fiberglass, nylon, and plastic parts turned into a crossbow with a two-hundred pound pull. It had been decided by Leighton and Blade that an old-fashioned weapon like this wouldn't arouse many suspicions in the Dimensions, and though the crossbow wasn't enough for a battle, it was more than enough to give not-too-subtle hints to even the largest and hungriest carnivore or human hunting party.

Blade slung the crossbow across his chest where Cheeky had been, and Cheeky climbed into the space in the ruck-sack where the crossbow had been. This kept Cheeky safe and Blade's hands free. He still didn't have quite the free-dom of action he'd had before he teamed up with Cheeky, but Cheeky was not only a friend and companion, he was also an extra set of eyes and ears. He pulled his weight; if a human companion did as well, Blade would have no com-plaints.

Secure with his weapon and companion, Blade almost felt like whistling as he set off toward the river.

It took longer to get down to the riverbank than Blade expected. It had been around noon when he emerged in this Dimension. It was close to midafternoon when he finally knelt down by the cold, gurgling water. While Cheeky kept watch, Blade drank and refilled his collapsible plastic canteen, then watched while Cheeky drank. After that they picked a convenient boulder that gave them a good view in all directions, from the riverbank to the tree-covered hillsides on either bank. Blade unslung his ruck-sack and started sorting through the contents.

It was pretty much the same amount he'd taken on his last trip—freeze-dried food, spare clothing, a sleeping bag, and a disposable cigarette lighter made entirely of plastic. There was also a plastic pocket compass, and aside from the magnetic compass needle, the only metal he was carrying was the blade of his knife. It was a U.S. Marine Kabar, not as elegant as his old commando knife but a lot more useful for chopping up kindling, gutting fish, and dressing game. Again, it was not a very incriminating piece of equipment.

Everything was in the right place and in good condition. Blade would have been surprised if it hadn't been. The Project's Field Operations officer was a former Royal Marine Commando who knew how a leaky cigarette lighter could be a major disaster if you were a long way from home.

Finally he took off his belt and wrist bracers, and inspected them. They looked like they were made of ordinary pliable plastic from Home Dimension, but it actually was a very special sort of plastic. It was Oltec from Kaldak, part of the harness of the uniform Blade wore back from that Dimension on his second trip.

Normal plastic softened when heated and hardened when cooled. This plastic worked the other way around. Thrust into boiling water, the belt and wrist bracers hardened until they were nearly as tough as steel and much lighter. Laid on a block of ice or immersed in cold water, the plastic softened until Blade could shape it between thumb and forefinger and then put it back on. Most of the plastic was still in the laboratories of the Project's Complex Two, being analyzed. Blade had kept enough for the specially designed belt and cuffs, which, when straightened out and hardened, became a spear and two daggers with sharp points. He could be wearing nothing but his bare skin and the innocent-looking plastic, and still hold a dozen men's lives in his hands. Cheeky wore a harness and belt of the same material.

Blade took off his wrist bracers, straightened them out, held each piece over the flame of a cigarette lighter, and watched them begin to harden. Suddenly Cheeky gave a soft *yeeep* of warning. Blade looked up, and saw that he and the feather-monkey were no longer alone.

Chapter 3

A number of dark-skinned men were climbing down the slope of the far bank of the river, moving sure-footedly from the cover of one boulder to another. They were closing in on both sides of the mouth of a canyon that opened on the riverbank. The canyon's floor was level but it twisted so sharply that Blade could see barely fifty yards into it. From somewhere up the canyon a cloud of dust rose.

Blade counted at least twenty men. Fortunately all their attention seemed to be on the mouth of the canyon. Blade's camouflage coveralls were also doing a good job of hiding him against the dark gravel of the riverbank. He easily found cover for himself and Cheeky before the men reached the bank of the river.

The men's skins were brown with a tinge of bronze, and their hair long, dark, and glossy. Most of them wore nothing but sandals and leather loinguards; some were completely naked. The ones with loinguards seemed to have daggers thrust into their belts; all carried spears with wicked-looking barbed heads and tufts of feather at the butt ends. Some had their hair tied up with vividly colored headbands. More than anything else, they made Blade think of a hunting party of North American Indians before the white man came.

The dust cloud in the canyon seemed to be getting

closer and thicker. Now Blade could hear an occasional bel-
low and the echoing rumble of many hooves. The hunters
hurried out onto the open ground along the bank and
divided into two parties, one on each side of the canyon
mouth. Each party formed a line that reached from the
base of the slope to the water's edge. All raised their
spears, and those with daggers drew them. The sound of
hooves swelled to a roar.

Then suddenly the canyon spewed out a solid mass of
furious animal life. In the lead were a dozen shaggy animals, looking like oversized elk—except that no elk ever
had a rack of antlers like these. The antlers were a deep
red, at least seven feet from tip to tip, and so massive
Blade wondered how the creatures ever managed to keep
their heads up. He could have chinned himself on either
side of such a rack! Finding themselves suddenly in the
open, the elk slowed down and began to mill around, bellowing to one another.

Five of the dark-skinned hunters rode out of the canyon
after the elk. The hunters were mounted on creatures that
obviously must have had lizards somewhere in their family
trees. Their scaly bodies weren't much larger than a Shet-
land pony's, but their thick legs were a good five feet long
and ended in splayed, clawed feet. Their eyes swiveled like
a frog's, but when they opened their mouths they dis-
played a fine set of teeth. The hunters rode bareback, with
only ropes for bridles, and carried ten-foot lances or spiked
clubs. Blade wasn't sure if these weapons were for their
prey or to control the strange-looking members of the
hunting party that were bringing up the rear.

There were four of these creatures at the heel of the
hunters. They were hairy humanoids that reminded Blade
of the legendary Sasquatch or Bigfoot.

The smallest was at least seven feet tall and four feet
across the shoulders, with arms reaching almost to its
knees. Both hands and feet were clawed, and their long
muzzles were studded with teeth. Great clumps of matted

brown hair sprouted all over them like weeds. Blade even caught a whiff of their rank odor, which made him perfectly happy to watch the end of the hunt from a distance.

The lizard-riders slowed their mounts and urged the Bigfeet forward with high-pitched cries and prods from their lances. The Bigfeet threw back their heads and bellowed. Blade recognized the noise; he'd heard it from down in the first canyon. He realized he'd narrowly escaped meeting a den of these creatures in the wild. Then the Bigfeet shambled forward in a crouch that was almost a parody of a karate adept's stance.

Now the elk panicked again. Some of them ran left or right, straight at the hunters waiting for them. Blade saw a hunter stand up, ignoring the lowered antlers coming at him until the last moment. Then he leaped aside, catching the antlers in one hand and swinging himself up on the elk's back. Before the elk could figure out what to do next, the hunter stabbed it at the base of the neck. The elk reared in one desperate twisting convulsion. The hunter flew off but landed on his feet as lightly as a gymnast, avoiding the elk as it crashed to the ground.

The other elk were too confused to run. Or perhaps they thought the Bigfeet were less dangerous than the human hunters. They were wrong. Blade saw one Bigfoot leap on an elk's back and jerk its head back until the neck snapped. Another grabbed an elk by the antlers, threw it to the ground, then tore out its throat. A third waited until the elk in front of it reared. Then it struck with both hands, claws outstretched. The elk's belly opened in a wound six feet long, and steaming entrails poured out as it fell. The Bigfoot knelt down by its victim, feeding on the entrails even before the elk was dead. A lizard-rider rode up beside the Bigfoot and not too gently prodded it away with a lance.

In a matter of minutes all the elk were dead or dying except two. One had the sense to run back up the canyon; two of the lizard-riders went after it. The other ran at the right-hand line of hunters, with one of the Bigfoot after it.

A totally naked hunter stood between it and escape. He raised his spear and made a half-hearted thrust. The spear caught in the elk's thick hide and the animal's speed wrenched it out of his hands. He took a couple of steps after the elk, then jumped back as the Bigfoot headed toward him. For a moment it looked as if the Bigfoot thought the hunter was its prey, and the young man froze, staring at the Bigfoot. That moment was long enough to let the elk through. With open ground ahead, it broke into a run.

Blade saw that its course was going to bring it right opposite him. He unslung the crossbow, dropped a bolt into place, and had it cocked and raised by the time the elk was in range. Sighting carefully for a head shot—he didn't trust anything else to bring down such a large animal—he counted to three, took a deep breath, and squeezed the trigger.

The elk stopped as if it had run into a stone wall. Then it shook its head, and for a moment Blake feared he'd shot only a glancing blow. As he snatched another bolt from his belt he saw the elk stagger, then topple sideways so violently that part of its antler broke off. As he finished reloading, the elk gave a final twitch, then lay still.

It was a minute or so before anyone on the far bank noticed either Blade or his work. They were all standing around the hunter who'd let the elk through, or else guarding the dead elk from the Bigfeet. Blade used this time to quickly disassemble his crossbow. He didn't want to take the chance of arousing anyone's suspicions. At last someone looked along the bank and saw the last elk lying dead for no apparent reason. He did a perfect double-take and started looking around frantically for his gods only knew what. It was then that he saw the tall man standing on the far bank of the river. He started waving his spear and let out a screech that sounded to Blade like a cat with its tail caught in a door.

The others promptly did the same. Blade held out both hands, palms outward, in the standard gesture of peace. As long as the hunters were only waving their spears instead of throwing them, Blade was inclined to give them the benefit of the doubt. Even if they did start throwing, the closest man was a good fifty yards away.

Eventually several of the hunters put down their spears and matched Blade's gesture. One who appeared to be in command pointed upstream, then pointed at himself and the men around him. Blade assumed he was indicating a way to cross the river, so he picked up his bow and told Cheeky to climb aboard.

They reached a ford about half a mile downstream, clearly marked by water boiling white around half-submerged rocks. Blade was glad the river was no more than knee deep here, since the water was icy cold and flowing fast.

Three of the hunters met him on the other bank, all with loinguards and daggers. Seen close up, they looked even more like American Indians. They didn't look too well fed—not exactly starved, but with no fat on their lean and sinewy frames. They also smelled as if they hadn't bathed since the day they were born.

The hunters were silent and impassive all the way back to the main party. Blade began to wonder how he was going to be able to communicate in the local language if they didn't *say* anything!

Normally the transition into Dimension X affected Blade's brain so that he understood the local language as English and the natives understood his English words as their tongue. This phenomenon probably had something to do with telepathy, and certainly Blade would have been dead a good many times over without it. He was good at learning languages, but not *that* good.

By the time they got back to the main party, the two

riders who'd chased the elk up the canyon were back, triumphantly waving bloody lances. Everyone else was busily at work, skinning and cutting up the carcasses into manageable chunks. Off to one side, a pile of guts and bones grew steadily.

The man who'd seemed in command came up to Blade, walked around him several times, then sniffed at him like a dog. He said nothing, but Blade could make out enough of the conversation among the hunters to know he'd be able to understand the local language as well as ever. That didn't mean he could understand what it was they were talking *about*, but that was always a separate problem.

Finally the leader frowned. "Are you of the Idol Makers?"

Blade shrugged. It was his habit in new Dimensions to go along with whatever story was suggested to him. "I have not seen your Idol, so I do not know if it is the work of my people or not. It would not be lawful for me to look upon your Idol without your leave."

This show of respect for their taboos went over well. The chief smiled and nodded. "This is so. Indeed, you would need more than my leave to look upon the Idol. The Wise One of the Rutari must look upon you first."

"Will you take me before the Wise One?"

The chief laughed. "I think she would have me thrown to the Great Hunters if I did otherwise. There is great magic in you; your weapons-magic is powerful. The Wise One seeks to know all she can of magic, wherever it comes from or whatever its purpose, and she will want to know if your magic is good or evil."

"Then she deserves her name."

At this point the chief seemed to notice Cheeky for the first time, peering over Blade's shoulder. He raised a hand in an obvious gesture to ward off evil spirits, and several of the hunters raised their spears. Before anything more could happen, an earsplitting burst of squeals, roars, and growls made conversation impossible.

The Bigfeet—the Great Hunters—were feeding. Turned loose on the pile of bones and entrails, they were squabbling over the tidbits, punching each other, cracking bones for the marrow, and throwing away anything they didn't want. The chief led Blade away from the Great Hunters until they could talk without shouting or being hit by flying bits of elk gut.

"Is that a—a First Friend, like the Wise One's Moyla?" the chief asked, pointing to Cheeky.

"Again, I cannot say. Certainly I had other friends before I met Cheeky, but we are close and do each other much honor. He is part of my magic, and I am part of his."

"Then indeed he is very like Moyla," said the chief. He seemed to hesitate. "Is there a name I may call you, that will give away none of your magic?"

"Among my people there is no magic in a name alone," said Blade. "So my true name is my only name. Call me Blade."

"To give away your true name and not fear losing much of your magic must mean that the magic of your people must be as strong as that of the Idol Makers, even if you are not of them," said the chief. "Will you forgive me if I do not do the same?"

"Certainly," said Blade. "You have no reason to trust me *that* much."

The chief laughed. "I have a very good reason to trust you." He pointed downstream to where Blade's kill lay. "Whatever else may be said of your magic, it has done good work for the Rutari this day."

"I thank you," said Blade. As he'd expected, he'd got off on the right foot with these people—the Rutari?—by adding meat to the tribal larder. Hunting peoples never had so much food that a little help in getting more didn't go over well.

"You may call me Teindo," said the chief. "Now, do you know the art of dressing out one of the Red-Horns, or may one of our hunters aid you? If there is shame—?"

"There is no shame in admitting that my magic does not tell me how to do everything," said Blade. "In my own land I have hunted ones like the Red-Horns, but not the same. I would not waste the meat or the hide of the Rutari's Red-Horns out of mere pride."

"You are long past your first kill, I can tell," said Teindo. "Are you a Blue Hunter of your people?"

"No," said Blade. "Hunting is not my true work. My work is to travel to distant lands and seek out the wisdom of the people living there."

"Giving them something in return, of course?" said Teindo. He was still smiling, but his eyes were suddenly hard.

"Of course. I said I was a traveler, not a thief." Teindo laughed. Then Blade continued. "I can travel faster and farther if I gather my own food as I go. I was taught by the Blue Hunters of my people, though I am not one of them."

At a signal from Teindo, a young naked hunter, one of the Red Hunters, stepped forward. Blade signaled Cheeky to hop down, unslung his pack, and started taking off his own clothes. Dressing out big game was a messy job, he had few changes of clothing, and the nearest laundry was a long way off.

When Blade was naked he put his clothes in his rucksack and walked three times backward around the pile, reciting the words of "Rule, Britannia" in pig latin. This seemed to impress Teindo and the other hunters as a proper spell. So did Blade's explanation.

"I have changed the magic of my weapons and other things so that it will not reach out against the Rutari. However, the magic is still there, ready for anyone who touches anything without my leave. I do not doubt the honor of the Rutari, but once a people whose honor I did not doubt stole my weapons. I nearly died, and since then I trust more to my own magic than to anything else."

Teindo looked at Blade's collection of scars. "No man

who has fought as many battles as you have can offend me by being careful.''

Blade picked up his Kabar knife in one hand, and whistled Cheeky up onto his other shoulder. Then he led the young hunter off toward the dead Red-Horn.

Chapter 4

Cutting up an animal the size of one of the Red-Horns with only two knives was as long and bloody a job as Blade had expected. Cheeky kept a safe distance from the whole thing. He was a rigid vegetarian, barely able to tolerate even the sight and smell of so much meat.

By the time he'd finished, it was nearly dark, and the Great Hunters had long since gorged themselves and fallen asleep. So had some of the hunters, including the one who'd flinched aside from the charging Red-Horn. He was sleeping a little apart from the rest of the hunting party, Blade noticed. His spear was thrust into the ground near his head, and the tuft of feathers had been removed from the butt.

Blade made a separate bed after going through an improvised ritual over his clothes and equipment. Once you got started on a reputation as a wizard, you had to keep up the act until somebody allowed you to abandon it. Blade wondered if the Wise One would grant him that freedom before he ran out of things he could use for incantations and spells!

Apart from this, his stay in this Dimension seemed to be off to a good start. The hunters of the Rutari didn't seem ready to stab him while he slept, Cheeky was with him, and he had food, water, and the promise of an introduction to a local potentate. Best of all, nobody appeared

to know the Dimension X secret from a sack of fertilizer or
care about finding out! After the return to the Dimension
of Kaldak, he'd have slept soundly enough with nothing
going for him but that!

A messenger with word of the great kill of Red-Horns
had left for the Rutari village before dawn. A whole caravan of the lizard-horses returned by early afternoon, some
of them ridden by women. The women wore as little as
their men, and some of the younger ones were more than
good-looking, if a trifle on the lean side.

Everyone turned out to sling the meat in nets of lizard-
hide thongs on either side of their mounts, wake up the
Great Hunters (who were still sleeping off their meal of
the night before), and clean up the campfire. By the time
the caravan was ready to leave, there were no traces of the
Rutari camp left except bloodstains.

"Seldom do our enemies, the Uchendi, come this far
into our lands," Teindo explained. "But Those Who Have
Gone Before watch everywhere. They do not honor care-
lessness or other weakness—" with a glare at the young
man who'd flinched. "If they thought we needed a lesson,
then they might allow the Uchendi here."

As they marched, the Bigfeet were again kept way in
the back, in the care of several lizard-riders who prodded
them from time to time and kept them moving and in line.
Blade was marching in the rear of the line of hunters, along
with the young hunter, whose name turned out to be
Awgal. "You have done nothing to prove yourself weak
like Awgal, Blade," said Teindo. "But until we are sure of
your strengths, you must march with him."

"I should say that I have done much to prove myself
strong," snapped Blade. Among primitive peoples,
letting yourself get pushed around wasn't just embarrass-
ing; it could be fatal. You always had to tread a fine line
between being polite and being self-deprecating.

"So you have—I think," said Teindo. The conversation

appeared to embarrass him. "But only the Wise One can be *sure* that you are strong in the ways that make you fit to be truly one of us."

"I do not like this," said Blade coolly. "The Cheeky does not like it either. But it is not worth fighting over. Do you swear that no harm will come to me, from Awgal's presence, if the Wise One judges me strong?"

Teindo swore this so earnestly that it was hard for Blade to keep a straight face. At last Blade said, "Very well. But I warn you. If there is any curse on me from marching with Awgal, I will not just turn it away from myself and the Cheeky. I will send it on to *you*, and you can tell the Wise One why you need her help to take it off!"

Teindo gulped but nodded. "So be it, Blade."

With the lizard-horses heavily loaded and most of the people on foot, it took until evening of the next day to reach the main village of the Rutari. Blade had hoped that Awgal would talk freely to him on the way; outcasts and criminals frequently were his best sources.

However, Awgal apparently feared that if he talked to Blade, either the Wise One's magic or Blade's would make his already bad situation worse. Or perhaps it was just that he didn't feel kindly toward the wizard who'd slain the Red-Horn he let escape. Blade got about six words out of Awgal during the whole march.

They reached the village at sunset, passing along a river valley sown with grain and vegetables. Apparently the Rutari weren't completely dependent on hunting: however, Blade noticed the soil was quite stony.

The Bigfeet were led away to the lair where they were kept when not on hunting expeditions. Then the meat was unloaded and hauled to a cave that exhaled clouds of mineral-smelling steam. The Rutari preserved their meats by salting and boiling it over natural hot springs deep in the cave. That made sense to Blade. Hauling loads of

firewood on lizard-back over rough mountain trails was
something anyone would gladly avoid. After unloading the
meat, most of the hunting party scattered to the welcome awaiting them in the huts, which were set on the
sides of the valley, clear of the cultivated land. Teindo and
six other hunters led Blade and Awgal uphill to the most
remote hut of all, to meet the Wise One.

If the Wise One was more than forty, she was very well
preserved in spite of her gray-white hair. She wore an
embroidered leather skirt, boots with leather tassels
around the top, and a complicated headdress of something
that reminded Blade of porcupine quills. She was bare to
the waist, and Blade could see two long scars on her
smooth brown skin, one across her stomach and the other
down her left breast.

Perhaps it was the scars that gave her such a forbidding
appearance. Or maybe the total lack of expression in her
wide gray eyes. Either way, Blade was sure from the
moment he entered the hut that the Wise One deserved
her name. Keeping up his cover story with her was going
to be a challenge, one he'd better be able to meet. She
looked quite willing to have him thrown to the Great
Hunters if she thought he was lying.

Blade was so intent on studying the Wise One that he
didn't notice her pet until Cheeky went ''*Mreeep!*'' and
pointed toward the gravel floor of the hut. Sitting beside
the Wise One was a creature that seemed to have a mon-
key's body and a cat's head. The fur was brown and long
enough to curl, the eyes nocturnal, and the delicate paws
busy playing with a strip of leather. When it saw Cheeky,
the animal made a faint hissing noise, then dropped the
leather and scurried behind its mistress. She reached down
to stroke it until it was silent, then looked back to Blade.

''What you are, no one has told me, not even Those
Who Went Before. So we must learn for ourselves. As for
you, Awgal, there is nothing strange about you or what
you have done. However, I must still be as wise about you

as I can be, before I give judgment. In the presence of the Spirits, I must find out if you were truly weak. Now take this." She picked up a handful of what looked like dried red peas from a bowl in her lap and handed them to Awgal. He seemed reluctant to take them.

"Will you eat of the *kerush* as you're told, or do you ask that I pronounce judgment without knowing all I should?"

Awgal grunted. "What have I to lose?" Teindo and the other hunters glared at him for this defiance.

"If you think you have nothing to lose, then you are not only weak but foolish, Awgal. You know how the Great Hunters kill."

Awgal grunted again. "I do. But I would rather lose my life to them than to you."

That defiance was too much. At a signal from the Wise One, Teindo and the other hunters knocked Awgal down and rolled him over on his back. For a moment Blade thought Awgal really was going to lose his life to the Wise One; she had a knife in her hand.

She only used the knife to threaten him, holding it against his neck. Then she held his nose until he had to open his mouth, and popped a handful of the *kerush* beans into it. He choked, gasped, tried to spit them out, but finally swallowed them. A moment later his nostrils flared, then the pupils of his eyes began to contract.

By the time they'd constricted to pinpoints, his breathing was slow and shallow. The Wise One hitched up her skirt and knelt astride his torso, almost as if she were planning to ride him sexually. Instead she placed one hand on each temple, closed her eyes, and controlled her own breathing until it was exactly in time with the hunter's.

Blade's attention was on the Wise One when Cheeky interrupted his thoughts. The mental picture he sent left Blade sure what was happening. According to Cheeky, the *kerush* was making Awgal send his thoughts telepathically, and the Wise One was reading them.

Suddenly the Wise One's pet hopped up on her stool, hissing, squeaking, lashing her tail, and waving her arms furiously in the direction of Cheeky. The hunters who were free to move stared at the two animals, then started to move toward Blade. He dropped into karate stance and got ready for a fight.

The Wise One jumped to her feet, so abruptly that her knees rammed into Awgal's stomach. He doubled up, gasping and wheezing. Her sharp gesture to four of the hunters made them pick up the helpless man and carry him out. The Wise One turned to face Blade, glaring at him but holding her knife as if she wasn't entirely sure she was still in control of the situation.

"My pet and I heard you and the Cheeky doing wizard work or *kerush-magor* in my presence!"

Blade shrugged. "I don't know what you mean by this." Would the Wise One of the Rutari, an honorable people, accuse me of doing something I did not do?"

"*I* am the judge of the honor of the Rutari, Blade!"

"Then speak as a wise judge, and not as one who fears spirits roaming in the night. If I did wrong it was without knowing that it was wrong. If that means nothing among the Rutari, then I ask myself—*are* they an honorable people?"

Blade knew this blunt appeal to the Wise One's notions of honor might be taken as an insult, and if it was, he'd have a devil of a fight on his hands. Teindo and the other two hunters were armed, and the Wise One herself was no weakling. Blade doubted he could fight without someone getting killed, which would mean he'd have to leave the Rutari, not to mention the secret of the *kerush* and its effects on telepathy. It seemed that every time he was on the edge of discovering something vital, he ran into someone's hot temper or tribal taboo!

Apparently unable to think of anything better to do, the Wise One sat down on her stool again, then laid the knife in her lap and crossed her hands over the hilt. The silence lasted so long that Blade wondered if she'd withdrawn into a telepathic trance again. Finally she looked up.

"I judge that you did no harm, and indeed did not know that you were doing wizard work, or *kerush-magor*. Still, you must be cleansed by the Great Hunters before you come to *kerush-magor* in my presence. And Awgal, the Red Hunter, has shown weakness in the presence of the Spirits of the Hunt; the Spirits demand that he be cleansed before he is allowed in their presence. Those Who Went Before demand the same."

"And I shall be cleansed as Awgal? If that is your judgment, I would rather die here. I think I can do a better job than he did of defending myself." He'd measured the distance to all of his prospective opponents and knew he could have two of them down before they could move.

The silence dragged on, and the tension mounted. Just as Teindo seemed about to open his mouth to shout for help, the Wise One's pet began squawking and hissing indignantly. Then it hopped up on its mistress's shoulder and put both paws on her forehead. They stayed like that for a minute, reminding Blade very much of himself and Cheeky having a particularly intimate telepathic conversation.

In fact, that was probably what they were having. Blade only hoped that Cheeky could resist the temptation to eavesdrop again, even though the "pet" had to be the Wise One's "First Friend," Moyla, and could let them in on some important information.

Finally the Wise One smiled thinly. "You will face your cleansing from the Great Hunters as you came from your mother. But you will face only one, and you will face him on your feet, with all your strength and wits as they are."

So he was not going to be tied up or drugged until he

was helpless, then devoured by the Great Hunters. That was something. Maybe quite a lot. And if he could secretly carry a weapon . . .

"May I have the Cheeky standing beside me, so that he may be cleansed, too?"

"Is he your First Friend?"

"No."

"Teindo says you told him he wasn't. But—if he is not your First Friend, then what is he?"

"A friend of a sort not every man has. I can say no more."

"I hope he is a very rare sort of friend indeed. Otherwise he shall be hardly more than a mouthful for a Great Hunter." She waved her knife at Teindo. "Take them to the caves."

Blade let the hunters lead him and Cheeky out. So far, so good, was his feeling. He'd proved that he was ready to fight for his honor and for just treatment. He'd even given himself a chance of learning more about the telepathy of the Rutari.

Now all he and Cheeky had to do was survive a bare-handed duel against one of those hairy nine-foot monsters. Or almost bare-handed, at least . . .

Chapter 5

The morning of Blade's cleansing before the Great Hunters was his fourth in the village of the Rutari. The two hunters and two young women who guarded him awoke him even earlier than usual, and offered him a lavish breakfast. Boiled eggs, porridge, fried beans, a thick stew, dried fruit, thin beer to wash it all down—enough for three hungry people Blade's size.

He couldn't quite keep out of his mind thoughts about the condemned man eating a hearty meal. He'd worked out his plans carefully and in as much detail as he could, using every scrap of information gleaned on the Great Hunters and the place of the cleansing.

Only when Cheeky could be persuaded to stop thinking of Moyla was Blade able to work things out with him. The feather-monkey understood what was at stake, but Blade could only hope Cheeky's odd ''crush'' on the Wise One's familiar wouldn't affect his loyalty.

It also wasn't reassuring that Blade didn't know if the Wise One could hear his telepathic conversations with Cheeky. If she overheard him, she certainly would know a good deal Blade would rather she didn't.

He'd thought of probing his guards about the use of telepathy among the Rutari and their enemies. This ran him straight into his old problem: How much could he ask without giving away the fact that he was familiar with telepathy himself? That was one thing he would be just as happy the Wise One didn't know for a while!

Blade thanked his keepers so generously that the girls started to giggle, and the hunters glared at them. Until he'd survived his cleansing and been examined by the Wise One he was taboo for the women of the Rutari. The girls were willing to flirt, but they weren't willing to do anything that might lead to their facing the Great Hunters.

Despite the quantities of food served him, Blade ate lightly and made Cheeky do the same. Both of them would need all the speed they had against a creature that could probably rip Blade limb from limb without even breathing hard. Blade could no longer eat, drink, and make love all night and then go out to face half a dozen opponents quite as easily as he had when he was fresh out of Oxford. His travels in many countries and Dimensions had left their mark.

It was a clear, brisk morning. Blade, Cheeky, and his escort tramped swiftly down the valley to the sacred field at the bottom. The hills around the field made it a natural theater for the day's performance, and Blade quickly saw there was going to be no shortage of spectators. What looked like half the Rutari people were busily finding themselves places on the hillsides. Most of them carried skins or furs to sit on and leather bottles or hollowed-out gourds of beer. Some carried baskets of food. The general atmosphere seemed more like a holiday than a solemn religious occasion.

It struck Blade that the more the people drank, the more festive they'd feel and the more they'd appreciate a good show. He and Cheeky would do their best; having the crowd on his side might save his life.

The pit of the cleansing itself was about a hundred yards across, steep sided but with a level floor covered with short wiry grass and patches of gravel. On one side gaped the black maw of a cave; Blade caught the familiar carrion reek of a Great Hunters' den. In the middle of the pit stood a black stone pyramid with a ledge carved on one side. Even from a distance Blade could make out the ancient bloodstains on the stone. Beside the pyramid, steam rose from the mouth of another of the valley's numerous hot springs. If it was as hot as all the rest Blade had encountered, it would be more than hot enough for his purposes.

A drum began to thud slowly from somewhere up the valley, and the festive atmosphere quickly cooled. A few latecomers scurried in, while mothers and older daughters rounded up straying toddlers and shushed them to an uneasy silence. Then a short procession wound its way into sight around the flank of the next hill up the valley.

First marched six warriors wearing loinguards and carrying spears. They were led by Teindo. Next came four more warriors, carrying Awgal on a litter piled with moss and leaves. His head had been shaved and painted green. From his blank stare, it looked to Blade as if he was either drugged or scared out of his wits.

Then came the Wise One herself and a young woman—a very good-looking one, Blade couldn't help noticing. She seemed to be a sort of assistant or acolyte to the Wise One, carrying Moyla in a bag on her chest and a sack full of gourds, sprigs of herbs, and other magical gear on her back. Six more warriors, all naked, brought up the rear of the procession.

As they marched down into the pit and up to the pyramid, Teindo, as first among the Blue Hunters, was called on to pass Awgal into the hands of those who had the true knowledge of cleansing. First among these was the Wise One of the Rutari, who had a long list of other titles as well, though Blade had never heard her personal name mentioned. No doubt the Wise One had enemies so potent that it was unsafe to let her true name be known. Tiendo struck the pyramid three times with the feathered butt of his spear. Then he turned to the Wise One and delivered a short ritual speech:

"Let the Wise One perform the cleansing of Awgal. I call on the Spirits to witness, that I, Teindo Blue Hunter, have done my duty." The Wise One made three passes over Teindo's head with her carved staff of office. Then she laid some herbs on the ground and set them on fire, and Teindo leaped three times through the smoke. Finally he led the other warriors up out of the pit to join the guards around Blade.

Through all of this Awgal sat on the litter, gazing vacantly into space. Now the Wise One approached him, straddled him, and seemed to give him another telepathic message. He slowly rose from the litter, moving like a disjointed puppet, and stumbled to the pyramid. With a little help from the two women, he lay down on the ledge.

Now both women took off their skirts and stood naked at the base of the pyramid. The Wise One poured something from a gourd into a clay cup, and the acolyte handed it to Awgal. Obedient as a child, he emptied the cup. From the sighs and whispers around him, Blade guessed his cooperation was a good omen.

After a minute or two Awgal began to stir—at least in one part of his body. The potion in the cup was obviously a potent aphrodisiac. The acolyte waited until Awgal reached the appropriate state of arousal, then positioned herself and slid down into place.

Awgal's face remained stonelike as the young woman rode him to one climax after another. The acolyte's face was more expressive. She might be doing this as a religious duty, but she was also having one hell of a good time doing it! Time after time her body twisted and convulsed, her head thrown back so far that her fine breasts with their erect nipples were pointed at the sky and her long black hair practically brushed Awgal's feet. In spite of the chilly morning, sweat was pouring off her, and after a while she could no longer be silent. Her sobs and groans floated out over the valley.

Blade would have been more interested if he hadn't remembered what was going to happen to Awgal as soon as the acolyte got through with him. This didn't bother some of the people around Blade; there was a good deal of public fondling going on—very public, considering how little everyone was wearing. One or two couples were actually down on the ground.

Under the influence of the aphrodisiac, Awgal's endurance exceeded the young woman's. At last she rolled off him, crawling down the pyramid on hands and knees, groaning with exhaustion and unable to stand. Again sighs and moans indicated this was a good omen.

Now it was the Wise One's turn. She knelt over Awgal and performed fellatio on him for a while. Then she took her acolyte's place and rode Awgal until she'd climaxed three times. The last time, Awgal's face showed that he was feeling everything too. When the Wise One let out a final cry of release, Awgal groaned happily. That seemed to be still another good omen, although by now the sighs of good omens were a little hard to tell from the sighs of pleasure and passion.

If this was supposed to be a cleansing, Blade decided, it was certainly thorough in at least one area. Awgal wouldn't have a sexual thought for a week, if by some chance he lived that long.

In fact, he had no more than a couple of minutes left. The mood of the crowd changed abruptly as a bellowing scream from a Great Hunter echoed from the cave. Four warriors emerged from the shadows, leading one of the beasts and controlling it with knob-headed staves. It was a small Great Hunter, no more than seven feet tall, but Blade had no doubt it could do the job. He firmly told his stomach to sit tight and prepared to watch Awgal's end.

After all the long preliminaries, Awgal died mercifully
fast. The two naked women had barely time to scramble
up on to the top of the pyramid before the hunters
released their charge. The Wise One frantically snatched
open a gourd and poured its contents over herself and her
acolyte as the beast charged toward them. It leaped halfway up the pyramid without breaking stride, then recoiled
from the two women as if it had run straight into a brick
wall. Blade caught a whiff of what the Wise One had
poured out and didn't blame the beast; *he* would have
recoiled from any food or female smelling like that!

The Great Hunter slid back down to the ground, roaring
in rage and frustration as it lost its balance. It was up
again in a moment, sniffing around. A long sigh went
through the crowd as the beast scented Awgal and turned
toward him.

Then one clawed hand came down like a butcher's
cleaver, tearing Awgal open from ribcage to groin. No
drugs could dull that kind of pain; he gave a horrible
bubbling scream and sprayed blood all over his killer. Then
the Great Hunter picked him up like a torn-apart rag doll
and smashed his skull against the stone hard enough for
Blade to hear the *crack* that put Awgal past feeling any
more pain.

The Wise One shouted something and waved her staff;
so did the four warriors. The Great Hunter grunted several
times, then grabbed Awgal again. Apparently the rite
called for the victim to be devoured in public, instead of
carried off to the cave. As hunger won out over whatever
else the creature was feeling, it tore off one of Awgal's
legs and started gnawing on it.

The rest of the feast was just as gruesome as the killing.
By the time Awgal was reduced to a pile of bloody frag-
ments, Blade was glad he'd ordered his stomach to be
quiet. The only consolations were that the Great Hunters
apparently killed fast, and that at the sight and smell of

Awgal's death, Cheeky hadn't lost his nerve to follow through with their plan.

Blade did allow himself one small hope. It would be nice if the Rutari cleaned up what was left of Awgal before putting him into the pit!

Chapter 6

The warriors led Awgal's killer back into the cave. Apparently each candidate for cleansing got a fresh beast. Blade would have been happier to fight Awgal's killer, not so much for vengeance but because a Great Hunter slowed down by a heavy meal would be less formidable. Also, he'd rather face a seven-footer than a nine-footer—its reach would be shorter. Little details—but Blade could hardly remember a time when he hadn't been aware of them and used them in his plans as naturally as he breathed. Being an essentially practical man, he didn't spend much time wondering why this was so; he was alive and healthy because of the habit, and that was enough for him.

Under the Wise One's supervision, a dozen men and women cleaned the pyramid with buckets of water drawn from the hot spring. By the time they'd finished, the whole pit was filled with steam and smelled of sulphur and the herbs the Wise One threw out in handfulls while the others worked. Then the Wise One raised her staff and pointed toward Blade.

Blade rose, and Cheeky jumped up on his shoulder without needing a signal. Blade grinned and sent a picture of him and Cheeky standing beside the corpse of a Great Hunter. This was the first real life-or-death battle he and Cheeky had fought as a team; he hoped it would also be the first of many victories. The sensation of not having everything depend on his own strength, speed, and wits was odd but agreeable.

At the rim of the pit, Blade was solemnly inspected by the warriors for signs of any clothing or weapons not allowed by the rules. They practically ignored Cheeky, and completely ignored the feather-monkey's plastic harness. Blade heard one say, "If he wants his good-luck pet with him . . ." but nothing else.

Blade went down into the pit so quickly that the guards had to scramble to keep up with him. One of them lost his footing on the slope and slid the rest of the way down on his rump. Murmurs of approval for Blade's confidence mingled with laughter at the guard. A good start, Blade thought.

The Wise One called Blade to the foot of the pyramid and asked him a series of ritual questions, waving her staff and throwing handfuls of herbs about while she did. Blade answered the questions as quickly as he could without seeming disrespectful. As long as he had to look at the Wise One, he couldn't study the floor of the pit and check the footing it offered him.

However, there was always Cheeky, who would know what to look for. If Blade could just send him a brief mental message—*very* brief—without the Wise One "hearing" . . . Well, why not try it once?

Blade sent Cheeky a picture of him jumping down and running around, poking at the gravel and grass, picking up stones and pulling up tufts. Cheeky *yeeeped* and obeyed the implied order. The Wise One's staff and herb throwing never missed a beat.

Cheeky couldn't have been more thorough if he'd been searching the pit for jewels. He even threw a handful of pebbles into the hot spring to see what would happen. A cloud of steam gushed up, and he jumped back, squeaking indignantly.

At last he finished his inspection, and the Wise One was still asking Blade questions. Was she trying to trip him up in public, make him say something ill-omened so that he would have to be "cleansed" like Awgal? Blade hoped not. He might fight his way out, but he'd have little chance of saving Cheeky. That meant he wasn't going to get out of here at all if the Wise One wanted his blood. He would never leave Cheeky; they were going to live or die together.

Even if the Wise One didn't want his blood, this interrogation was buggering up his survival chances. As long as it went on, Cheeky couldn't report what he'd learned. The Wise One would notice Blade's attention wandering elsewhere, then ask why.

In fact, Blade realized that he couldn't even see Cheeky anymore. He couldn't imagine the feather-monkey running off in fright, but if the Wise One suddenly decided his presence here was against the law and custom . . .

Then a small feather-crested head appeared over the top of the pyramid, between the Wise One's feet. Blade forced himself to go on talking, but also got ready to move fast. Now Cheeky was up on top of the pyramid, and the Wise One still hadn't noticed him. If anyone else saw him they didn't seem ready to warn her.

Then Cheeky leaped forward. Someone shouted, someone else cursed, but both were too late. Cheeky leaped up—and tweaked the Wise One's pubic hair.

The Wise One let out a shriek and clapped her hands to her groin. This left her completely defenseless against Cheeky, who swarmed up her body as if it were a tree. He planted his hind feet on her breasts, gripped both shoulders with his forepaws—and kissed her on the nose.

For a moment Blade was surrounded by the awesome silence of a thousand people all holding their breaths. He hardly breathed himself, and didn't dare move anything except one hand, in a signal to Cheeky to come back down and join him.

Then the silence fell apart as the thousand people dissolved in laughter. Blade let out his breath in a long *whoooosssh*. The little bastard had certainly been gambling for high stakes! If the Rutari had taken his antics as a breaking of taboos . . .

But they hadn't. They'd taken it as a good joke on the Wise One. Her own pride should keep her from ordering Blade killed or sacrificed now. Of course, she might have a few notions about what to do some other day, but Blade believed in living through each day as it came.

Cheeky responded to Blade's mental message, leaping down and hurrying back to his master's shoulder. He left the Wise One to recover her staff and as much of her dignity as she could manage. By the time the laughter died, she'd succeeded, and her acolyte had joined her on top of the pyramid.

Cheeky took advantage of the Wise One's distraction and reported his findings to Blade. The water in the hot spring was more than hot enough. The stones of the gravel were too smooth and fine to hurt Cheeky's paws. The footing was solid. Blade could not be slowed down—but neither would the Great Hunter.

Blade did not much care for the look in the Wise One's eyes as he turned his back on her to face the mouth of the cave. The acolyte, on the other hand—well, if she was still looking at him that way after the cleansing, he might take her up on the offer. He'd be in better shape to enjoy it than Awgal!

Blade's Great Hunter burst out of the cave at a dead run, spraying gravel as it came, its deep-set eyes fixed on Blade. The creature was closing in, and there was no time for analyzing anything. Cheeky jumped down from Blade's shoulder and ran one way. Blade ran the other. Blade was silent, while Cheeky made as much noise as he could. From what he'd overhead among the hunters, Blade knew the Great Hunters traced their prey mostly by sound and scent, not relying much on their poor eyesight. Cheeky was a lot smaller than Blade, but he could make as much noise, or more.

Blade's guess was the right one. The Great Hunter swerved after Cheeky, bending low and reaching forward. It seemed to realize vaguely that its prey was smaller than usual. As the clawed hands opened to scoop up Cheeky, the feather-monkey reversed course and dashed between the Great Hunger's legs. He got clean away, and for a moment the beast was off balance, its back turned to Blade.

Blade came up behind it in a leaping side-kick, driving his left foot into the small of its back. The foot had all of Blade's speed and two hundred and ten pounds behind it. Any human being's spine would have snapped like a matchstick. But the Great Hunter only staggered, then straightened up with an indignant grunt.

Blade felt as if he'd kicked a tree. He was reasonably sure he hadn't broken his foot. He wasn't sure he hadn't bruised it so badly it would swell up before the fight was over and slow him down.

For a moment, though, Blade still had all his speed. As the Great Hunter lurched around to face him, he chopped hard at the nearest wrist. Damaging one of the creature's hands couldn't hurt. Indeed, it couldn't hurt the Great Hunter: Blade had the feeling that he'd tried to chop through an iron bar.

In return, the Great Hunter lashed out with its other hand in a casual gesture, apparently intending to shoo Blade away like a fly rather than to inflict injury. The blow sent Blade flying over backward. If he hadn't known how to fall, he might have landed hard and stayed down until the Great Hunter finished him off. As it was, he landed rolling, made a complete somersault, and came up facing his opponent more or less in one piece. He was fairly sure his ribs weren't broken. He did suspect torn muscles and was sure of torn skin. Three parallel gashes were bleeding freely.

He'd better use his speed to stay out of the Great Hunter's reach for a while. Otherwise there were going to be more bleeding gashes in his skin, and not such neat ones either. He sent this message to Cheeky as well. He suspected that Cheeky would have much less trouble evading than he would. The feather-monkey could practically turn around in his own length, and he was much harder to detect as long as he kept quiet.

The crowd was now silent, their laughter at the Wise One's embarrassment long past. The sight of a man pitted against one of the Great Hunters with nothing but his own strength and wits and perhaps his pet to aid him was nothing to laugh at. The Wise One and her acolyte stood on top of the pyramid, their long hair now lifting to a slight breeze, their faces unreadable. Blade hoped that whatever the Wise One was thinking, she would stop short of giving the Great Hunter telepathic coaching on the fight. Then he and Cheeky settled down to their dance of death with the beast.

Once he'd decided firmly in favor of caution, Blade was able to keep his distance, not without danger but at least without skating along the thin edge of disaster again. The Great Hunter was strong enough to take on six men in a close grapple, and incredibly fast when running in a straight line. It couldn't turn fast, however, and its eyesight was definitely poor. It practically ignored Cheeky, except when Blade told the feather-monkey to make enough noise to draw the beast's attention and give his master a little time to breathe.

Since he'd started with the crowd on his side, Blade knew he had a while before anyone suspected him of being a coward. And as much as he wanted the goodwill of the Rutari, he would go right on keeping his distance from the beast for as long as he had to. He and Cheeky simply didn't dare confront a Great Hunter with its full strength and speed left. One of those clawed hands would connect, and even if it didn't kill Blade outright it would do so much damage that the next blow could finish the job. The good-will of the Rutari would be of no use to a stone-dead Richard Blade.

The crowd began to buzz with excitement at the show Blade and Cheeky were putting on, circling around the pit. Snatches of conversation he overheard when Cheeky was drawing off the beast led him to believe this Great Hunter was a famous killer, and that he was doing something extraordinary by lasting so long against it.

If this was true, no doubt it would help after the fight—if there was an "after." By now Blade had more doubts about the outcome of this fight than he'd had about any for years. The Great Hunter seemed to have the endurance of a diesel locomotive, rather than a creature of flesh and blood. Cheeky was definitely tiring, and Blade himself was slowly losing blood from his three cuts. Before much longer he would be weakened or slowed down even without taking any more damage from the Great Hunter.

Before that happened, he would have to strike at least one damaging blow. It wouldn't be wise to use his planned trick with Cheeky this soon, so he would have to think of something else, fast. Having eight feet of sudden death, fanged, clawed, and steel-muscled, thundering at his heels will make any man think faster. Blade's wits now worked like one of Lord Leighton's smaller computers, and came up with a possible solution.

At Blade's order, Cheeky began squeaking and squalling to draw the Great Hunter off as he'd done before. The bait worked as well as ever. The huge beast plunged after Cheeky, who scurried along before it, paws scrabbling frantically on the gravel.

The Great Hunter was only a few feet out of reach when Blade cut across in front of it at a dead run. He had scooped up fistful of gravel from a patch of stones that were large enough to hurt. As the Great Hunter stooped, Blade hurled the gravel into its face. The beast howled so fiercely that several women in the audience screamed in

terror. Then the beast clawed at its eyes. It kept after
Cheeky, though, so Blade didn't assume it was blinded.

At Blade's signal, Cheeky fell silent and darted sideways. Blade shouted, whooped, and cursed, drawing the
Great Hunter after him, toward the hot springs. Cheeky
ran on ahead, around the hot springs, and on the far side he
started squeaking again. Blade fell silent as he reached the
edge of the spring, then flung himself into the air in a running broad jump, hoping it would take him clear across. If
it didn't—well, the Great Hunter would dine on boiled
meat today.

Blade's gamble on his remaining strength paid off. He
landed on his feet, scooped up Cheeky, and kept on running. Behind him the Great Hunter reached the edge of
the spring and also jumped. It was longer-legged than
Blade, but not built as well for jumping. Also, it was
jumping without a good view of the far side. It cleared the
spring but landed clumsily on its back, howling with new
rage and pain.

When it got up, it seemed to be limping and favoring
one arm. The crowd shouted in fierce delight, and some of
them stood up to see better. The Wise One waved her
staff at these eager ones, and they subsided.

Meanwhile, unnoticed by anyone, Cheeky had unhooked
his harness and handed it to Blade. Blade knew he could
never do serious damage to the Great Hunter without
some sort of weapon. Now he was about to get one. He
quickly took the harness apart and gave Cheeky the sec-
tion that would harden into an effective dagger, sharp
pointed and sharp edged, with a short handle. Cheeky
leaped toward the spring to harden the dagger in the hot
water, while Blade dashed off in the opposite direction to
keep the Great Hunter on his trail.

The beast was definitely slowed, perhaps in pain, and
certainly even angrier than before. At intervals it stopped
to pound its chest, let out bloodcurdling screams, and hurl
gravel at Blade. It never found stones heavy enough to

carry far or hurt much if they did hit. They usually didn't; Blade's attack hadn't done the creature's already dim eyesight any good.

However, the Great Hunter still had both arms in working condition and was moving much too fast for Blade's peace of mind. He was glad to see Cheeky darting away from the spring. The feather-monkey held the dagger aloft with his tail curled around the hilt, using all four paws to run. He reached Blade, raised his tail until Blade could take the dagger, then opened the distance between himself and his master.

The audience was completely, almost oppressively silent. The Wise One's face was still a stone mask, but the acolyte was leaning slightly forward, her full lips parted.

Blade and Cheeky darted toward the Great Hunter from opposite sides. As Cheeky approached he cried out. The Great Hunter stopped, undecided on which prey to seize, both arms outstretched. One hairy wrist was in reach of Blade's knife. The Kaldakan plastic, hardened like steel in the hot spring, slashed down. Fur, skin, and flesh gaped open to the bone, blood spurted, and an unearthly cry of rage, pain, and surprise echoed around the pit. Several hundred human voices joined the uproar.

The Great Hunter was still formidable. It turned toward Blade, lunging with its good arm. Blade sprang backward but not far enough. The hand came down on his left shoulder, fortunately without driving the claws in. Blade twisted free, feeling as if his shoulder were dislocated or his left arm out of its socket. Before the Great Hunter could move again, Cheeky closed in.

He swarmed up the creature's hairy back and gripped its neck with his hind legs and tail. Then he brought his forepaws around and clamped them hard over the creatures eyes. The Great Hunter howled again, shook its head in frustration, and raised its good hand to pluck away this annoyance.

That left Blade with a clear path. He lunged in and up

· with the dagger. The sharp point drove into the creature's right eye. It nearly took off a couple of Cheeky's fingers as it did, but the point drove deep. The Great Hunter lurched, jerking the dagger out of Blade's hand, and Cheeky leaped free. The creature lunged again, and went down on its knees, both hands groping blindly ahead of it, blood pouring from the slashed wrist.

Blade put both hands on the creature's shoulders, vaulted on to its back, got both arms around the massive neck, and jerked with all his strength. His arms nearly came out of their sockets, but the neck snapped with an entirely satisfactory noise. Then the Great Hunter went limp. Blade staggered to his feet, and all the Rutari around the pit started yelling themselves hoarse.

Blade bent down and picked up the dagger, then pulled out a handful of the dead Great Hunter's coarse fur to wipe the sweat and blood off his skin. Then he saw the matted filth in the fur and threw it aside. He stood silently, until blood and sweat together made a puddle in the gravel at his feet and the shouting died. Considering the exhaustion, loss of blood, strained joints, and narrowness of his victory, Blade would much rather have done almost anything else than to have fought the Great Hunter.

Oh, to lie down and be plied with massages and wine by six beautiful girls. He spat to clear the dust from his mouth and brushed the hair out of his eyes. *Next time, if I have to choose between fighting a Great Hunter or going for a ride in a cement mixer, I'll take the cement mixer.*

Then the acolyte was running toward him, all dignity and ceremony forgotten. She threw her arms around him and kissed him, and he was suddenly very aware of both his nakedness and hers. She was warm in his arms and smelled sweet even under the stink of the herbs and potions.

Fortunately the Wise One came down into the pit before Blade and the girl could forget he was still taboo. The Wise One was smiling now, but it was an odd, enigmatic smile. Blade would almost have preferred a glare of open hatred. Then he would have known where he stood. As it was, the Wise One was as much of a mystery as ever.

Chapter 7

The celebration of Blade's victory in the cleansing started almost as soon as he staggered up the side of the pit, with the acolyte on one side and Teindo on the other. It went on all that day and well into the next. Things didn't get back to normal among the Rutari until the day after that, when the last hangover wore off. The Rutari's home-brewed beer was crude, but there was a lot of it, and from somewhere they'd acquired the art of distilling. Their liquor was even cruder than their beer, but Blade couldn't deny that it was potent.

Everyone seemed to have forgotten Awgal, or at least be unwilling to admit that they remembered him. It was as if the young hunter had never been. Blade held his peace. There was more of his cleansing to come, and until it was finished he was neither fish nor fowl among the Rutari.

Not that he wasn't tempted to throw caution to the winds, surrounded by nearly naked young women who made it obvious they wanted him on their sleeping mats as quickly as possible. Blade lost count after the first dozen. None of them seemed to give an empty gourd for the taboos, and some of them said as much in plain language. Apparently war and hunting were so much more dangerous than childbirth among the Rutari that the adult women outnumbered men at least two to one. So unmarried

51

women were as free as the air, and most married women were in polygamous households.

Teindo had three wives, all of whom seemed to have something of a reputation among the women of the Rutari. He finally drove all the other women away from Blade by warning them that his wives had been promised first chance at Blade when he was lawful. Any woman who got to Blade before them—well, he might help them after they were killed for breaking the taboo, but he would do nothing for them until then. The hovering women and girls couldn't have vanished faster if Blade had suddenly turned into a Great Hunter and devoured one of them.

"I thank you, Teindo," said Blade, offering him a gourdful of liquor.

"It was my duty to save those women from unlawful beddings. The consequences would not speed up what remains of your cleansing."

"And where is the Wise One?" Blade asked.

Teindo looked at the ground. "She has gone before the Idol, to seek its answer before she completes your cleansing."

"Does she expect one?"

"Who can speak truly of the Wise One's mind, Blade? And who would dare speak of the Idol's will, save her?" The warning was unmistakable.

Blade decided to take it. "Not I, certainly."

"You are not too drunk to be wise, Blade."

"If a man's wits cannot survive much strong water, he does not live to travel as far as I have."

Teindo seemed satisfied with that answer. Blade accepted a few more congratulations, then returned to his hut. He'd have liked to find out what the Wise One thought of her humiliation at Cheeky's hands, but suspected that anyone who knew wouldn't tell him.

However, Blade had long known that the best thing to do about something you couldn't predict was sleep on it. He curled up on his furs and fell quickly and soundly asleep.

In fact, he not only slept but snored so loudly that Cheeky woke him up several times during the night, squawking indignantly about the noise.

The Wise One spent several more days consulting the Idol of the Rutari, longer than usual. Blade saw Teindo beginning to look worried, and when he looked at Blade, suspicious. Blade made up his mind that if the Rutari tried to confine him he would assume the worst, and he and Cheeky would make a run for it, stark naked if necessary. He wasn't curious enough about telepathy to risk Awgal's fate.

Cheeky assured Blade that he saw eye-to-eye with his master on the matter of running. Blade would have been happier if Cheeky hadn't also been sending out so many mental pictures of Moyla, the Wise One's First Friend. He seemed to have a real passion for her.

At first Blade couldn't avoid thinking that this passion was completely ridiculous. Cheeky was indignant, and managed to get across the message that it was all a matter of what you were used to. Blade had to admit there was sense in Cheeky's argument. If he himself was two feet tall and covered with feathers, Moyla might indeed look like the sexiest thing on four feet!

He still wished Cheeky hadn't fallen in love with Moyla. She might not give two straws for him, and that would be bad. Even worse, she was the loyal familiar of a formidable telepath, who might easily be Blade's and Cheeky's deadly enemy when she returned from the visit to the Idol. How do you convince a feather-monkey from another Dimension that he's about to become a security risk? How do you even explain the concept to him?

At last the Wise One returned. Teindo himself brought word, and also the woman's summons to Blade to appear before her the next morning. Teindo's face was unreadable; Blade could not tell if he was being summoned for execution or to be crowned king of the Rutari. Until the Wise

One spoke for herself, the best he could do was keep his eyes and ears open, his mouth shut, and his back to a good solid wall.

"Enter, Blade," said the voice from inside the hut.

Blade recognized the Wise One's voice. Neither he nor Cheeky had made a sound except for his footsteps; Blade wondered if she read his mind or just made a lucky guess that it was him outside the hut, hoping to frighten him if she was right. Blade pushed through the hide that covered the door and strode in.

Without waiting for the Wise One's permission, he picked a corner of the hut and sat down cross-legged. Cheeky jumped down from his shoulder but stayed close by. From his corner Blade could see the whole hut by the glow of the fire on the hearth in the middle, but he himself was in a shadow. And just as important, nobody could get behind him.

The Wise One and her acolyte, also cross-legged, sat by the hearth. Both wore leather skirts and necklaces of what looked like gold nuggets strung on leather thongs; the Wise One also wore a fur thrown loosely over her shoulders. Their gourds and sacks of potions and herbs were piled nearby, and their smooth skin shone in the firelight as if they'd been rubbed with oil.

The Wise One smiled as Blade took his place in the corner, but said nothing until he'd made himself comfortable. Then her smile widened. It looked almost friendly, as if she really felt no ill will toward him. The acolyte's smile was even wider, but of course Blade knew what she felt toward him.

"Welcome, Blade, to the other part of your cleansing, which is to partake of the *kerush*. May you do as well tonight as you did the day you faced the Great Hunter. And you need not sit there as if I might call up Those Who Went Before to snatch away your spirit. I can do you no harm with the *kerush-magor*—the wizard work—unless you call evil up yourself by trying to fight me.''

Blade frowned. She might be telling the truth. Even if she weren't, this might be a good time for plain speaking. He caught a brief mental message from Cheeky: The feather-monkey feared a quarrel between his master and Moyla's mistress. Blade replied with a weary hope that Cheeky would get over his case of the hots for Moyla, then turned to the woman.

"That is easy for you to say, Wise One and—do you have a name, most lovely lady?'' to the acolyte.

"You may call me Ellspa.''

"Thank you. As I said, it is easy enough for you to tell me that you will do me no harm with the *kerush-magor* in this, the other part of my cleansing. But do I hear the truth?''

"Yes.''

"I know nothing to make me sure of that, Wise One.''

"What do you know to make you doubt it?''

"Little enough. But I have lived as long as I have only by not putting myself into the power of those I do not know. To submit to taking the *kerush* would go against all I have ever learned.''

"You cannot live among us uncleansed,'' said the Wise One. She sounded more sorry than angry about this.

"You seem very sure that I want to live among the Rutari,'' said Blade. He raised a hand for silence as both women seemed about to speak at once. "That does not mean I wish to live among the Uchendi tribe, your rivals. It does not even mean I wish the Rutari harm. It only means what I have said—that I may not wish to live among the Rutari enough to give myself up to the *kerush*.'' Blade shifted his position slightly, ready to move fast if the Wise One's next words were a call to the guards outside.

The two women looked at each other for a long time in silence. Then the Wise One sighed. "Blade, it seems we have no power over you to make you do as we wish without our telling you the truth." He nodded agreement. "I thought so. But—to tell you the truth is to give you knowledge that might do the Rutari much harm in the wrong hands. It is knowledge that only those who have been cleansed—and not even all of those—are permitted to have. Can we at least have your oath, by whatever you hold sacred, that you will do the Rutari no harm with what you learn?"

"I can swear that I will tell none of it to any known enemy of the Rutari, certainly. I have been a guest among you, and in honor I owe you this much. I cannot swear more, because how can I know all of those who may be enemies to the Rutari? I cannot see the future, Wise One."

Ellspa grinned, but the Wise One looked embarrassed. "I am sorry. I spoke unwisely, asking more than the gods allow. I did not do this to trap you. Will you believe me, and forgive my unwise words?" She sounded genuinely apologetic.

"Certainly I will forgive you. If you will forgive me for Cheeky's—behavior—the day of my first cleansing?"

Blade thought the Wise One was blushing. Certainly Ellspa was holding her breath and biting her lower lip to keep from giggling. Then the Wise One nodded.

"Blade, no harm was done to me. I forgive you. And no harm will be done to you tonight. Now—will you hear me tell you why this is so?"

Blade settled himself more comfortably, and Cheeky hopped up on his lap. "We will."

Chapter 8

The Wise One's explanation was simple, compared to what Blade expected. In a nutshell, the Wise One suspected that Blade had the potential of high-grade telepathic powers, such as most of the Uchendi had. Very few of the Rutari had such powers, usually only the Wise One and a few others of each generation. This was true no matter how much *kerush* they took.

"More then a few of our people have died, seeking to become as the Uchendi through too much *kerush*," Ellspa added. "Even a Wise One has been known to go too far." The Wise One gave her acolyte a sour look and continued her story.

"Apart from their greater mind powers, the Uchendi are less than we are in all things pleasing to the gods. That is why we took the Idol from them. It cannot have been the wish of the gods that such weaklings find favor in the eyes of the Idol Makers, who were surely the chosen of the gods."

Another bloody tantalizing hint about the Idol Makers! Blade gritted his teeth against the temptation to ask about them. One broken taboo an evening was enough.

"Because the Uchendi are unworthy," the Wise One went on, "we must wage war against them until they are no more. Then the Idol will be forever safely in the place where the gods wished it to be. When the Idol Makers return, they will come straight to the Rutari and bless us.''

Blade gritted his teeth harder. Aloud, he said, ''And you think that my powers of mind are something I can teach you, so all the Rutari will be as strong as the Uchendi?''

''Yes. You are the first man who is neither Rutari nor Uchendi to give any hint of such powers. If you have them, and can teach them . . .'' The Wise One's lips were trembling. Obviously she felt the whole fate of her people was at stake in Blade's cooperation.

And if she feels that strongly about it, one slip and you're dead, Blade's training told him.

Yes, but consider how much I might learn, he replied. *If nothing else, they have the* kerush.

Which might destroy your mind.

True, but you've got to run a few risks in order to learn anything. And there's no danger to the Dimension X secret here. These people are centuries from having computers.

What about inter-Dimensional travel by telepathy?

What about it? I've resisted the telepathy of the Wizard of Rentoro, who could do it. If these people aren't at least as strong as he was, they're no danger to me, even with the kerush. *Even if they do wind up traveling to Home Dimension, what harm can they do when they get there? The Kaldakans had lasers. These people don't even have bows!*

I guess you're right. Go ahead, then.

''No honor the Rutari can give will be held back,'' the Wise One was saying. ''The storytellers will give your name to the children of the children of our children, and tell how grateful we were to you.'' Ellspa licked her lips.

Blade wasn't a complete stranger to ''recreational'' drugs. He'd been involved in a couple of experiments to test the usefulness of LSD in his work. Also, while doing undercover work, he'd smoked his way through enough marijuana to know that he much preferred good Scotch.

However, he'd never tried mixing telepathy and drugs

before, and would have preferred his first time to be under safer conditions. Since nobody gave a damn about his preferences, there was nothing to do but swallow the *kerush* seed and hope for the best.

Ellspa emptied a small sack of *kerush* seeds on to the floor in front of Blade and divided them into three equal piles. "These are the raw seeds," she said. "Chew them slowly."

It would have been easier to do this if the seeds hadn't tasted like oven-roasted peanuts dipped in roofing compound. Blade still obeyed, cautious about an overdose. By the time he'd swallowed the remains of the fifth seed, the first was beginning to take effect.

Blade felt as if he were sitting in thin air, several inches off the ground. His hands and feet were also separated from his wrists and ankles—he could see that clearly. Just as clearly, he could still feel them and control them. He could even pick up a sixth seed, chew, and swallow.

Then the Wise One raised her hand to warn Blade to stop, and she and Ellspa began taking their *kerush*. They took nine seeds apiece, faster than Blade. With one part of his mind he expected to see the two women float up off the floor like balloons. With another part, he realized that they were able to take a larger dose, or perhaps even needed it, with their greater tolerance built up over the years.

It was a relief for Blade to discover that the logical, rational side of his mind was still working. It was not quite so much of a relief to discover that he was getting an uncomfortably solid erection.

By the time the two women had finished their seeds, both were swaying gently, as if in time to inaudible music. Their eyes were wide, their breathing quick, and their mouths hanging open. Blade noted in an oddly detached manner that Ellspa's dark nipples were also erect.

Now Cheeky scurried between Blade and the women, then hopped onto Blade's lap. In Blade's present condition

that was the wrong place for Cheeky. Blade winced, and
Cheeky leaped up onto his master's shoulder.

(''You want female?'')

''What?'' Blade's surprise made him speak out loud. He
was hearing a voice in his mind, whether male or female he
didn't know, and he had no idea who was ''speaking.''

(''Use the spirit speech.'') This time it was not a question but a command. It also had a very different ''tone of
voice''—call it a *flavor*—from that of the original question. Blade took several deep breaths to improve his con-
centration. He considered and rejected the idea of using
mental pictures, as he did with Cheeky. Then as soon as he
could be sure of not using lips, tongue, or vocal cords, he
formed the words in his mind.

(''I have the spirit speech, if this is it. And I do want
the females.'') Actually he didn't really want the Wise
One, but it would hardly be tactful to say so.

(''Yes. Old female not like it that way.'')

(''Cheeky!?'') Blade's astonishment at realizing it was
the feather-monkey speaking almost caused him to leap up
and hug the animal.

(''It's me.'')

(''You took the *kerush*?'')

(''Yes. One seed.'')

(''We have better—telepathy—now?'')

(''Yes. You think—louder—now.'')

(''Much—louder.'') It was the other mental voice, the
one with the different ''flavor.'' Blade looked at the two
women. It had to be one of them, but which? And had the
Wise One heard him ''thinking'' that he didn't want
her?''

(''I am not offended, Blade. You are a young man, and
Ellspa is a young woman. I cannot make you other than
the gods have already done.'')

Blade was losing awareness of his body entirely now, as
the *kerush*-induced telepathic links with Cheeky and the
Wise One absorbed his whole mind. He was still conscious

of Cheeky's paws placed on his temples, and a mental message with Cheeky's flavor to it.

("I am to you like Moyla is to old female.")

("First Friend?")

("That my name?")

("Yes.")

("Then—I First Friend. Females not hear us now. You tell them I—First Friend.")

("Females—not good people. Should not know you are my First Friend, that we use spirit speech. That is a secret.")

("No secret! I First Friend. If females know I First Friend, they let me go to Moyla. You want females. I want Moyla. Moyla want me.")

Blade couldn't help wondering if that one *kerush* seed had also increased Cheeky's intelligence. Perhaps it was because they were communicating in words instead of images. Or was it that the increase of his own telepathic powers now let him hear thoughts that Cheeky had always had?

("You ask good question.") Cheeky had obviously "heard" the question in Blade's mind. ("Now, you tell females I First Friend, I give answer to your question. No tell, no answer.")

("You blasted little feather-covered blackmailer!")

Blade got the impression of wordless laughter, and the sense of a will as stubborn as his own.

("Blade, we cannot hear your spirit speech or that of the Cheeky. Is it there?") A new mental flavor, which probably meant Ellspa. ("Is this how you keep your oath?")

Blade wished there was a mental door he could slam— hard—in the face of both Cheeky and those two witches. Apart from the women not being able to listen in while he and Cheeky were in telepathic contact, the situation was getting distinctly hairy.

Cheeky's intelligence seemed to have whole new dimensions. The first thing the little bugger was doing was using it to blackmail his master into revealing important secrets. If Blade conceded this point—that is, to tell the Wise One he and Cheeky were like her and Moyla—and let Cheeky have his roll in the hay with Moyla, what next?

And if he didn't, also what next?

Another nasty question. A lot depended on Cheeky's cooperation, starting with the research into telepathy, which might salvage the whole Dimension X Project, possibly ending with Blade's physical survival here. But if Cheeky spent the rest of this trip sulking and was uncooperative . . .

Besides, Blade *liked* the little fellow. He didn't want to hurt or offend him. He let that thought flow through his mind and into Cheeky's as strongly as he could. Then he added:

("All right. I'll tell them that you're my First Friend, and you and Moyla can get your rocks off together. But if you ever threaten me this way again, it will be the end of us. You'll be turned over to Lord Leighton for experimental work, like the kind you had in Kaldak.")

A moment of stark terror, which told Blade that the threat had registered. Then a slightly contrite, ("Sorry. Will do like you want.")

("Good, Cheeky. Now take your hands off my head.")

The telepathic link with Cheeky faded. The one with the women grew stronger until it seemed that they were three bodies sharing a single mind.

("Cheeky is my First Friend. He also desires Moyla.")

("I am not surprised to learn this. Moyla has thought so for some time. Also, she has desired the—Cheeky.")

So Cheeky wasn't going to be turned down. Blade supposed this ought to make him feel better.

("Of course. Do you not wish the Cheeky to be happy, since you are apparently quite fond of him?")

("I am fond of him, and I do wish him to be happy. I also wish you would not speak so freely about every thought I have. I do not intend all of them for you. I hope this is no breaking of my oath.'')

Ellspa rested a hand on the Wise One's shoulder. Silence followed as the two women consulted privately. Then:

(''We admit you would not be breaking your oath, to have thoughts of your own. But under *kerush*, it is not the custom of the Rutari.'')

(''The customs of the English are not those of the Rutari. Do you wish me to be as one of the Rutari while I am among you?'')

(''That is a question with no easy answer. Certainly not an answer we will find tonight.'') The Wise One made a hand signal, and a stone fell out of the wall. It revealed a black hole and Moyla's face peering out. She saw Cheeky and stuck her head out farther, hissing softly.

Cheeky crossed the hut in three bounds, *yeeeping* in delight. Moyla reached down to help him, but he swarmed up the wall to the hole without any aid. He disappeared inside, and Blade rather hoped the *kerush* didn't make him sensitive to *all* of Cheeky's thoughts. After all, the little fellow did deserve privacy for his lovemaking!

Now Blade became aware that the Wise One had also vanished. Blade looked around the hut, but there was no sign of her. She must have gone as silently as a puff of smoke, and now here he was alone with Ellspa—and he suddenly noticed that she'd taken off her skirt. She sat cross-legged in front of him, naked except for her head-band.

Well, why not? Certainly his erection hadn't vanished. Quite the contrary. Blade felt as if he was good for at least half a dozen women, and here was only Ellspa, bare and smiling and probably more than ready . . .

It took no thought for Blade to reach out and stroke her cheek. She raised a hand and curled long fingers around his wrist. Her smile widened, and she shifted slightly to give him a better view of her breasts. Blade thought he'd never seen such breasts—small but perfect cones, with nipples his hands positively ached to touch, and his lips too. He moved closer, ran both hands down Ellspa's shoulders to cup her breasts—

Across the left breast he felt a raised ridge—scar tissue? Blade looked at the breast under his hand. To his eyes the skin was smooth and flawless. To his hand, though, Ellspa's left breast felt as if there was a long scar across it, running on up to the shoulder.

A long scar, like the one on the Wise One's breast. Somehow the Wise One had made herself appear to be Ellspa, Blade thought.

The eyes of the woman facing him widened. She had "heard" what Blade was thinking, and she started to get to her feet, angry that her ruse had been discovered. But Blade's hands, with a grip like iron, clamped down on her ankles and held them, then jerked her toward him. Herbs, gourds, and everything else scattered as Blade pulled the woman feet-first into his lap. Then his arms went around her, squeezing her so tightly that all the breath *wsssshed* out of her.

She fought in spite of this, clawing at Blade's back and trying to bite his ear. But her struggles only stimulated him more, and meanwhile he held her with one arm and ran the other hand up and down her back. It was a very fine back, straight and smooth, and there was no deception in her nakedness. She was as bare as a baby.

Now the Wise One abandoned her efforts to present herself as Ellspa and started trying to wither Blade's erection. She imagined them surrounded by howling cold winds, foul-smelling bogs, fires, monstrous beasts with jaws dripping slime and tentacles glowing obscenely.

Unfortunately she wasn't able to break Blade's grip. And as long as Blade was holding in his lap a woman like the Wise One, the only way she could have got rid of his erection was by castrating him. Just to make sure she wouldn't get that idea, Blade started projecting the thought of the two of them locked together, the Wise

One's slim legs clamped around his back, her lips flowing
wet and hot against him. . . .

The anger went out of the Wise One in a single moment.
In the next moment all the gruesome images faded away.
Her mouth was nuzzling the side of Blade's neck, with her
tongue licking his skin, while her hands went under Blade's
loinguard and practically tore it aside. Blade raised the
Wise One's head and kissed her hard, so that her lips
opened and her tongue crept out to meet his. Then, with
only the gentlest pressure of his hands on her shoulders,
she lay back on the furs and let him into her.

The pleasure at finally being there was almost explo-
sive. Blade didn't know how much was real and how much
was the Wise One's telepathic projections. He tried to fill
her with the image of her body writhing and twisting in
climax. If she didn't get there before what was left of his
control vanished . . .

Then there was no mind at all, only two bodies locked
together, arms and legs taking on a life of their own, lips
joining madly, then roaming up and down bare skin. Blade
lost track of the number of times the Wise One shrieked
and he groaned, because now it really didn't matter.

After a while he realized that the fire was burning low,
that the hut positively stank of sweat, and that the Wise
One was kneeling in front of him. Sweat was dripping off
her breasts—*her* breasts, no doubt about it, he could see
the scar. The deception was over.

Not the lovemaking, though. The Wise One bent over
Blade and worked on him with her mouth until he was
ready again. Then she sat back on her haunches to make
way for Ellspa to step up to Blade.

The real Ellspa? Blade waited until Ellspa had lowered
herself into place, then quickly ran his hands up from groin
to shoulder, fingers probing the fine skin for scars. They
closed over the lovely breasts with their stiff nipples, and
found no scars.

The real Ellspa. Blade pulled Ellspa down toward him

and put his lips where his hands had been. Ellspa rammed
her pelvis down against Blade's neck and clutched his
shoulders so hard her nails broke the skin. Then she cried
out, a long sobbing moan that lasted until Blade closed his
lips with hers.

A good start, Blade thought. Then Ellspa was moving
on him again, and Blade matched her movements with his,
because a good start was only half of it. The night wasn't
over yet . . .

Chapter 9

Blade never found out what kind of recommendation the Wise One and Ellspa gave his telepathy, but they must have spread glowing reports of his virility. In the next few days, it seemed that half the unattached women of the Rutari asked him for sex, and a fair number of the attached ones as well.

Blade tried to be a gentleman. He accepted as many of the propositions as he thought would be safe, mostly from the unmarried women. He'd proved himself in the *kerush-magor*, in bed, in the hunt, and in the pit against the Great Hunter, but not in war. Until he'd done that, at least some of the husbands would feel they couldn't honorably ignore his bedding their wives.

However, the problem of his having no reputation as a warrior looked like it was about to be solved. The air of the village was thick with rumors that the Rutari would soon march against the Uchendi. It would not be all-out war, but it would be the biggest raid in years against the ancient foe, with many prisoners for cleansing or other rites. There would also be all the chances Blade could ever want to distinguish himself as a warrior.

He might also find out more about the Uchendi. Everyone seemed to know two things: that their telepathic powers were better than the Rutari's, and that they were unworthy of keeping the mysterious Idol. If anybody knew anything else, they weren't talking. Piecing snatches of conversation together, Blade understood that the Uchendi lived in the plains farther down the River of Life, and depended more on agriculture than hunting. He also got the impression that they had better lizard-horses than the Rutari, but didn't tame or use the Great Hunters.

In a few more days, Blade saw men repairing harnesses and sandals, filling provision bags, sharpening spears and knives, and exercising lizard-horses and Great Hunters. The Wise One and Ellspa were busily supervising a large gang of workers of both sexes, cleaning the prison caves and laying in supplies of *kerush* and everything else needed for cleansings.

Three days before the raid was set to depart, Blade learned from Teindo that he would not be allowed to fight. To do him justice, the Blue Hunter seemed ashamed both of the messages and of having agreed to bring it to Blade. This didn't make him any the less firm in laying down the law to Blade, including promising him a harsh fate for disobedience.

"Being cleansed before the Great Hunters as Awgal was is the least you can expect if you disobey," Teindo said soberly. "There are other fates that might be yours, which I shall not describe. They are too ugly. Also, none of them have been used for so many years that I do not know all about them."

"Thank you for your kindness," said Blade.

Teindo ignored the sarcasm. "This is not my wish or that of either the Blue or Red Hunters. It is the wish of—those who think you have more to teach the Rutari than things about war.

"So—the Wise One says I'm too valuable to be exposed to Uchendi spears?"

"She has not said it exactly that way, but that is a good way of saying it, yes."

"Well, if the Wise One will punish any warrior who calls me coward, no harm will be done. If she does not do this there will be no peace between us. No one can ask me to hold my honor as a warrior lightly, no matter what they want to learn from me. This I swore before I left my own land, long before I ever heard of the Rutari or they of me!''

Teindo looked uneasily around as Blade raised his voice. But he seemed to be sincere when he replied, ''I will bear your message to the place from which I brought mine. Indeed, I do not think they are so foolish as to ask otherwise.''

''It is best that it be so,'' said Blade, and turned away to walk off briskly. His anger wasn't entirely an act. Was he a guest of the Rutari or a guinea pig for the Wise One?

Well, so much for his chances of learning about the Uchendi and their telepathy first-hand, unless he wanted to risk offending the Wise One. And he still didn't know much about telepathy among the Rutari!

The *kerush* would improve whatever telepathic powers you had, but how much it would improve was rather unpredictable. It would make almost anyone capable of receiving telepathic messages, in a muddled sort of way. He'd been to one orgy with everyone on *kerush* and knew just how muddled the messages could be. He and Cheeky communicated more clearly the first time they ever had a telepathic conversation! A fair number of Rutari could get up to the normal telepathic level of the Wise One and Ellspa with the help of massive doses of *kerush*. But the two women seemed to be the only really powerful telepaths in the whole tribe.

Blade might not have been so frustrated if he'd been able to talk freely with Cheeky. Unfortunately, Cheeky seemed to be spending all his time making love to Moyla and gorging himself on fruits and nuts the Wise One fed him. He was living a life of ease, and if he ever gave Blade or the Project a thought, Blade certainly didn't know it. He did know that Moyla didn't like him—she'd told Blade to ''Get lost!'' more often than he cared to remember.

Cheeky, Blade realized, was in the position of a boy in

love for the first time with a beautiful, willing, but rather dumb girlfriend. All his brains had flowed down into his sex organs, and were going to stay there for a while.

Cheeky sat on top of the hut of Moyla's mistress and watched the human fighters ride out of the village. Moyla was beside him and a bowl of nuts between them. They were his favorite kind of nuts, so Moyla got them from her mistress whenever she could. She did this sort of thing often, which proved to Cheeky that she liked him. It was almost the first time a female like him had felt that way.

The Master Blade did not like Moyla, Cheeky knew. He also knew that Moyla did not like the Master Blade. She thought he meant harm to her mistress, or perhaps would take Cheeky from her if he went away from the village.

Cheeky saw Blade standing in the shadow of a hut, watching the fighters ride past. Blade's face showed that he was not happy. Cheeky wished he could enter the Master's mind and find out more about his unhappiness. However, Moyla did not like spirit speech between Cheeky and Blade. When he tried to talk to the Master, she would be angry for days at a time.

If he could only learn how to reach his master to find out what he was thinking without either his Master *or* Moyla knowing! But he did not think he could do that without his Master's help in the first place. This was not good. Also, if his Master was angry with him about Moyla, would the Blade help him at all? The Master did not think like a female, but he seemed to think that he and Cheeky were as littermates to one another.

Perhaps if Cheeky brought to the Master some of what he wanted to know, he would forgive? Perhaps. What did the Master want most to learn?

Of course! The thing the Mistress Wise One called "the Idol." What was it? The Wise One herself had gone to it, taking Moyla with her. So Moyla should certainly know.

("I tell you about where I go, Moyla. Always I tell you.

Now you tell me about when you went with the Mistress to the Idol.'')

Moyla said and thought nothing. Instead she stroked Cheeky's crest in a way that always made him feel good and said she felt good, too. Then she cracked a nut and popped the meat into his mouth. He gave her paw an affectionate nip.

(''The truth, Moyla. You say I do what you do not want me to do. I say, you do the same. I want to talk. Where did you go?'')

(''You do not like me if you ask that sort of question. If you do not like me, I do not like you.'')

Cheeky glared at Moyla. She looked really angry, and all he could read in her mind was the anger. But there was something else there. She wasn't angry just because she thought he didn't like her as much as before. She was angry because she'd been told not to answer this question. If she'd been told this, then she must know the answer.

Again, Cheeky wished he could talk with the Blade about this. The Master was much wiser about asking questions, for it was his whole life. But the Master might not talk to Cheeky until Cheeky found the answer himself!

Cheeky was so angry he wanted to pull the feathers out of his head. He did not, because that would tell Moyla that he was angry, without her even reading his thoughts. Then she would tell the Mistress Wise One, and Cheeky knew the Wise One could spirit-speak to him whenever she wanted to even if he did not want to hear her.

That might be bad for the Master Blade.

So Cheeky decided he would do as well as he could with what Moyla told him without knowing she was telling him. That might be quite a lot, since most of the time she trusted him. Then, when he had learned everything he was going to learn, he would go to the Master Blade. The Master Blade was kind; he would understand why Cheeky had made his mistake and forgive him for it.

Then they would talk again as they had before. They

might even talk about what had come into Cheeky's mind, so that his thoughts seemed clearer and faster. There were old tales that at one time all the Feather People had been the way Cheeky was now. But the tales were so old that no one had ever met anyone who knew one of these Feather People with strong thoughts. Cheeky himself had never believed the tales, until suddenly his thoughts were also strong.

Surely the Master Blade would know more about this. If he did not, some other one of the Master People might know. The Master People always thought strong thoughts. They also lived much longer than the Feather People. Blade might have been alive in the time when the Feather People's thoughts were strong!

Cheeky stopped himself before he got so excited that Moyla would hear and then tell the Mistress Wise One about Cheeky's strong thoughts. That would be bad for him and for the Master Blade.

Chapter 10

Blade awoke with a swelling uproar from outside the hut in his ears, his head comfortably pillowed between a young woman's breasts, and one arm thrown around an older woman's shoulders.

He sat up and listened. He heard the trumpeting calls of the lizard-horses, the roaring and howling of the Great Hunters, war cries, cheers, and harsh laughter. He also heard an ugly undertone of screams of fear and pain. Once he heard a dreadful sobbing wail. There was despair in that wail—more despair than Blade thought any human being should ever have to feel.

"I think we have a victory," said the older woman.

"Victory?" said Blade. He wasn't entirely awake and alert yet. It had been a long but entirely pleasant night.

"Over the Uchendi. The warriors have returned with those to be cleansed," said the younger woman. "They are rejoicing. Let us do the same." She ran her hand down Blade's chest to his groin.

Gently he plucked her hand away. The noise outside was arousing his curiosity more than anything else. After a moment the young woman sighed. "Well, as long as the Wise One keeps you among us, it is not so bad. We will have other times together."

Blade grinned. "I thank you. But in time the Uchendi

73

must have their share of my attention, or I am no warrior. Now let me get out and see those I shall fight.''

Blade stepped out of the hut into a chilly gray morning and an uproar that was still getting louder. He headed for the nearest screams, rounded the corner of a hut, and saw his first Uchendi.

She was a girl who couldn't have been more than twelve, and she was being gang-raped on the stony ground by eight or ten Rutari men. Blood was running down her thighs, and one eye was already swollen shut. Somehow she still had the strength to scream.

Blade backed away hastily, before someone saw him and invited him to join in. He kept retreating until he was out of sight. He couldn't get away from hearing the girl's screams, until they died away to feeble moans and then into silence. Blade hoped this meant the girl was dead.

Two of the warriors tramped past, spears over their shoulders and satisfied grins on their faces. One of them saw Blade. ''You too late for the little one? We would not have left you out.''

Blade shook his head. He wanted to shake the warrior like a terrier shaking a rat. ''A girl that age—for my people she is not lawful.''

''Don't your people fight wars?'' said the other warrior. ''If you do, how can you make the victory complete if you spare women and children?''

''We have few women,'' said Blade, thinking fast. ''If we slew the women of other tribes, the first time we lost a war would be the end of us. The enemy would take all of our women and the tribe would die away. Haven't the Rutari ever lost a battle to the Uchendi?''

The warriors seemed to find the idea funny. They were still laughing as they went off—no doubt in search of an eight-year old boy to bugger, Blade thought sourly.

He didn't see any eight-year-old boys among the Uchendi prisoners, but he did see a girl about six being thrown to the Great Hunters. Fortunately she was dead. With wounds like hers, she *had* to be dead.

He also saw a good many Uchendi of all ages and both sexes being treated as their captors pleased. Most of what pleased their captors ran in directions that Blade suspected would have made the Marquis de Sade himself run screaming into the streets. The twelve year old girl was far from the worst. By the time he'd seen enough, Blade was very glad he hadn't eaten any breakfast.

The only Uchendi prisoners spared horrible deaths were six warriors who'd been captured more or less unwounded. They were being saved for a formal cleansing by the Great Hunters, and were under the Wise One's protection. That didn't keep them from being forced to watch their fellow tribesmen die horribly.

One of the warriors went beserk when he saw a Great Hunter devouring his son. He broke away from his guards, killing one and disarming another. With a stolen spear he plunged into the pit and attacked the Great Hunter. Catching it by surprise, he was able to run the spear into its chest before its claws disembowled him. He made no sound as he flew through the air like a doll and crashed down on the lip of the pit. Blade was close enough to see that the dead face was set in a triumphant smile. He himself felt like cheering.

It was small consolation to Blade to learn that the Rutari had taken many more prisoners than usual on this raid. They'd overrun a whole farming village before the alarm could be given, then defeated a party of warriors coming to the villagers rescue. After that, the Rutari retreated without having to fight again, so they'd won their victory very cheaply. They were feeling good, and the Uchendi were paying a horrible price.

Questions now plagued Blade. Should he stay with the Rutari and help the Wise One improve the tribe's telepathy? After seeing the brutality of the Rutari, he had no particular desire to help the Wise One give her people a decisive advantage in this feud. Then should he move on, maybe to the Uchendi or maybe clear out of reach of both warring tribes in this land of Latan?

Blade was in a quandary, but at the moment he had to worry more about the possibility of being called on at last to join the warriors in raiding the Uchendi and torturing the prisoners to death. If he didn't do both it would look suspicious, and he'd have to watch his back any time a warrior was within spear throwing distance. There were easier ways to spend a trip to Dimension X.

The Wise One might also pick some piece of military knowledge out of his mind as he was fighting. She herself was no warrior, but suppose she got an image of a bow and arrow, then described it to Teindo? He would know that it was a weapon that might give the Rutari a decisive advantage.

At the worst, Blade might wind up seeing the Uchendi exterminated, all because his knowledge of weapons had been communicated telepathically. At best, he'd wind up a closely guarded prisoner, certain to be killed if he made a single move to leave the village.

No matter how Blade looked at the situation, one bleak fact looked back at him. If he stayed with the Rutari, a lot of innocent people were going to die—horribly. So it was very simple; Blade would not stay.

Unfortunately there was a fly in the ointment. Or, more accurately, a flying feather-monkey. Cheeky didn't want to leave his new love, Moyla.

("Not good for her, I go," he said over and over again.)

("Not good for you, you stay behind—")

("Behind?")

Blade reshaped his thoughts to reflect Cheeky's limited vocabulary. It was growing rapidly, though, now reminding Blade of a bright seven-year-old's.

("You stay here without me. Then Moyla not like you anymore. Bad for you.")

("Moyla always like me. You think that cannot be. I think it can be.")

("You would.") Blade saw no point in arguing with Cheeky on the basis of his own experience with love. He was inclined to doubt declarations of undying passion, and also Cheeky's judgment.

("You not trust me?") Cheeky asked, having heard what Blade was thinking.

The devil take telepathy—far far away, and bury it! If Cheeky was really getting intelligent, perhaps it would be possible to teach him some manners about listening in on Blade's thoughts. But he wouldn't be teaching Cheeky anything if he had to leave him among the Rutari.

("You not trust me, Master?")

("No. You not think—strong thoughts, not *any* kind of thoughts. I trust you like—like a Great Hunter. It thinks only of food, you think only of Moyla.")

("If you not trust me, why I stay with you?") Cheeky sounded both angry and unhappy. Blade felt the same way, but had to recognize that the feather-monkey had some logic on his side. If Blade didn't trust him anymore, what could Cheeky hope to gain from the relationship?

("You no stay with me, if you think that way. Stay with Rutari, Mistress Wise One, Moyla. Be happy, if you can.")

("You, too.") Cheeky hopped down from Blade's shoulder and began collecting his gear. It didn't take him long—there was only his knife, plastic harness, and sweater. Cheeky pulled on both, and without a backward glance at Blade scurried out the door of the hut. Blade stood in the doorway until Cheeky was out of sight, and for a moment longer. Then he went back inside. There was nothing for him to do there, but he didn't want to stand where everyone could see him.

He hadn't felt so disgusted with the world since the day Zoé Cornwall, his Home Dimension girlfriend, had said good-bye because he couldn't tell her about Dimension X. Of course, Zoé had meant a lot more to him than

Cheeky—but Cheeky didn't have as good an excuse for leaving. It was understandable that Zoé would want a man who didn't disappear for months at a time without any explanation. All Cheeky had for an excuse was a bad case of the hots for Moyla.

Anger, grief, and disgust boiled over. Blade kicked a stool clear across the hut, so that it shattered against the far wall. Then he slammed his fist hard against the stone wall. Pain shot up his arm, and he saw that his knuckles were bleeding. He sighed, now disgusted with himself as well as with the world. After a bit, his mind started working again.

His best chance for leaving the Rutari was coming up within a few days, during the Hunters' Long Race. Fifty men competed in a sort of marathon, which took two days from start to finish. What could be simpler than to discreetly slip away during the race? With luck he could be so long gone that his trail would be too cold for even a Great Hunter to find before he was missed.

Then he would be free to head south to the Uchendi, without any suspicion falling on Cheeky. Angry as he was, Blade really didn't care for the idea of Cheeky's being thrown to the Great Hunters or cut up alive by the Wise One. Wiser beings than Cheeky had made fools of themselves and done more harm over love. Cheeky deserved the best chance Blade could give him to make a new life for himself here among the Rutari with Moyla.

But damn it, he was going to miss the little fellow! Cheeky had become a powerful barrier against the loneliness of Blade's life. He'd been that even before the *kerushmagor*. Now, just as Cheeky was becoming more intelligent, everything was ending.

No doubt Leighton would mostly mourn the loss of Cheeky's help in learning more about telepathy. Blade wouldn't quarrel with that. But he would regret much more the loss of Cheeky's friendship, both what had been already and what might have been in the future.

Chapter 11

The day of the Hunters' Long Race dawned cloudy and windy but dry. Blade would have preferred fog or even rain, even if it made parts of the race heavy going. Fog would hide him from the sharp-eyed Rutari hunters, and rain would diminish the Great Hunters' ability to smell and hear if they were sent after him.

However, here in the mountains it was early summer and the autumn rains were months away. He would just have to run like the devil and trust his luck and skill at evasion for the rest. The Rutari were undoubtedly good trackers, but Blade refused to believe they were supermen, even with the help of the Great Hunters and telepathy. And since the alternative to running was staying among the Rutari until his distaste for their customs betrayed both him and Cheeky—well, that was no alternative at all.

The starting line was at the bottom of the village, made of fifty carved stones, one for each runner. Blade studied the stones carefully. They were sacred, kept under the Wise One's care most of the year and only brought out for important rituals such as the Long Race. He'd also heard it said that these stones were carved in the shape of the head of one of the Idol Makers who had made great magic among the Rutari.

Unfortunately the stones were worn and the carving had

been stylized to begin with. He couldn't even tell if the stones showed a living creature, let alone the head of one, or what kind. So much for his last hope of finding out about the Idol Makers and the Idol before he left the Rutari!

At least the Uchendi would also know something about the Idol Makers. After all, the Idol had originally been theirs, before the Rutari declared a holy war on the other tribe and stole it. If Blade had better luck winning cooperation among the Uchendi from somebody besides lusty women . . .

The first leg of the race ran north, the second south. Blade planned to take leave of the Rutari on the north-bound leg. It would mean farther to go to safety, since the Uchendi were to the south, but it would also confuse the Rutari about what happened to him. They might think he'd suffered an accident and spend days looking for his body, while a live Richard Blade tramped south toward the plains.

The drum sounded to call the runners to their marks. Blade stripped off his clothes down to his loinguard and piled them in the sacred circle with the weapons and clothes of the other runners. He'd be leaving the Rutari in his bare skin and the Kaldakan plastic harness and wrist braces. He could only hope that the compass, knife, and other gear he'd be leaving behind wouldn't teach the Rutari too much. Cheeky might be able to explain some of it, but that wouldn't be entirely bad; it would earn the feather-monkey the Wise One's goodwill and make his position secure. He was no longer bitter about Cheeky's desertion; now he wished the feather-monkey as long and happy a life among the Rutari as he could reasonably expect.

The drums thudded again, longer and louder. Blade stepped up to his rock and began his warming-up exercises.

Ten miles into the race, Blade had to admit that he'd

underestimated the difficulties of his plan. It didn't help that much of the trouble really wasn't his fault. If he'd been allowed out of the village, he'd have got a better idea of what the race course was like.

The problem was that he'd expected to be out of sight of any other runner for many minutes, even an hour, at a time. It wasn't working out that way. So far he could see a good mile either way, and three or four other runners could always see him.

He had allowed for this—he thought he would simply move out so far in front that he'd have the course to himself. However, he hadn't expected most of the Rutari to be such good runners! Blade was a first-class long-distance runner; he'd kept up with Zungan warriors on their native plains, and run some of them to exhaustion. But he hadn't spent all his life walking and running over the rugged hills the Rutari called home. If he did manage to get out ahead, he'd be too exhausted to run much farther to escape.

Blade settled down to a pace he could maintain without strain, no longer trying to keep out of sight of his fellow runners. His legs moved like the pistons of an engine and his heavily muscled arms swung like pendulums, pumping the chill mountain air into his massive chest. Gravel sprayed out from under his pounding feet, and dust caked him where rivers of sweat didn't wash it away.

Rivers. That got Blade to thinking. The River of Life was the biggest and best-known river in the land of the Rutari. But it wasn't the only one. One of the others lay about two miles ahead, if Blade's memory served him right. Also, he recalled a hunter saying that the course of the race ran along cliffs beside the river for at least a mile. "A sure foot and a keen eye are needed there more than speed," the man said. "No man who fell into the Hungry Waters has ever come out alive."

That might be true for the Rutari, who were a hill folk; most of them could not swim. Richard Blade, on the other hand, could swim like a fish.

That was as far as he dared plan until he'd seen the cliff and the Hungry Waters. It still sounded like a good chance. He'd be breaking away in daylight, with plenty of time before dark, and he wouldn't have to spend days in Rutari land retracing his steps.

Blade settled down to his regular distance-devouring lope, as steadily as the ground allowed. Before another half mile, he felt the ground rising underfoot. Then it dipped through a stand of the blue-leaved trees. They exhaled an odd scent, like a cross between cinnamon and tar. Ahead, Blade saw the trail of a Great Hunter and beside the path a pile of its dung. No danger of attack here, though, with all the men alert and moving fast.

Beyond the trees the ground started to rise again. Within a hundred yards it was rising more steeply than anywhere before in the race. The path zigzagged back and forth up the face of a granite mass with a surface so rough even Blade's leather-tough soles felt it.

Then they were out under the open sky again, speeding along the cliff by the Hungry Waters. One look told Blade why the river had that name. The water boomed and roared dark and swift through a black-walled canyon more than fifty feet deep. At times it leaped over boulders, churning itself into foam. In a few places the foam turned into spray, veiling everything beyond.

Blade hoped what lay beyond wasn't waterfalls or rapids full of jagged boulders. This cliff really was his best chance, possibly his only one, and it wasn't going to last even a mile. Already he could see the first of the men ahead of him turning away from the Hungry Waters.

Well, here I go for the Rutari High Diving Championship, he thought, looking for the best place to jump. There was a nice pool just ahead, but the cliff above was so solid nobody would ever believe he'd stumbled. Just beyond that, though—

It would have to do. As Blade approached the overhang, he drew his hand across his eyes, as if sweat was beginning to blind him. Then he started to weave back and forth, getting a little closer to the cliff's edge each time. He heard a shout of warning from a man behind him; his act seemed to be working.

Up onto the overhang itself now, Blade found the footing slick and unpredictable; the spray was reaching high here. He took a longer step than usual, judged his distance, and let his right leg collapse under him.

The man behind shouted again as Blade toppled off the overhang and plunged into the Hungry Waters.

It was going to be dark soon. Cheeky hoped the Mistress Wise One and her friend Ellspa would be through talking before it was. Moyla said bad Spirits walked in the night, and the Wise One could call them up. So if the Mistress grew angry with Cheeky, she could do bad things to him much more easily in the darkness than in the light.

There was nothing Cheeky could do about it, though. So he sat in the corner and listened to the talk between the women. They were not using the spirit speech but were talking out loud, which made it hard for him to understand. But one of the things that had come to him with the power to have strong thoughts was the power to remember anything he heard, even if he did not understand. He wanted to remember what he heard now, because the Master Blade would want to know about it—if the Master Blade was still alive. The women knew more about that than Cheeky did, but even they were not sure.

"Who has ever come out of the Hungry Waters alive, in all the time since there were Rutari?" said the Wise One. She seemed angry with something or somebody, perhaps Ellspa.

"No one."

"Then why do you think Blade is the first?"

"I have a sense about him, that he is not as other men.

His coming means something for the Rutari. I do not believe he will die until we know what that is.''

''You dream, Ellspa.'' The Wise One was smiling, but she did not seem to find Ellspa's words really funny. ''And I think what you dream of is having the Blade back in your furs for a long time.''

''Perhaps,'' said Ellspa.

''Then why do you wish us to send hunters into all the valleys and up all the hills to seek Blade? If he's alive and they find him, he may still have done some unlawful act that will send him to the Great Hunters. Then you would get no pleasure from having him—''

Now it was Ellspa who was angry. Cheeky was certain of that, because she was sending out anger so strongly. ''I am not ruled by my loins the way you seem to think, Wise One. If Blade has done evil, then let him be punished. If he has done good, then so much the better. But I cannot imagine that he has done *nothing*. I will go alone into the mountains myself rather than admit that.''

''I will forbid you to do any such thing, Ellspa.''

''You may forbid. Can you stop me?''

''I can certainly do so more easily than Blade could have lived in the Hungry Waters.''

''I have learned more than you think, Wise One. You might not find me easy to stop.''

''You would challenge me, at a time like this, when you yourself say that there is danger for the Rutari?''

''Yes, I would challenge you, if I was sure you did not deserve your name.''

The two women were now glaring at each other, their arms and legs stiff, and their minds both sending out anger. Cheeky thought of two cats about to fight. He sensed that Moyla was unhappy about this, and put a hand on her shoulder to comfort her. He had no thoughts of himself now that he was concerned for her.

The anger between the two women lasted for a little while longer. Then the Wise One put her arms around

Ellspa and showed grief. "Ellspa, I am sorry. Perhaps you have had a true vision. But I do say that you are as yet too young to be able to know this for certain. Shall we go together before the Idol and ask *it* what has happened to the Blade?"

Ellspa smiled and kissed the Wise One. "Yes, we can go before the Idol. Since we took it from the Uchendi, it has always given us wisdom, in gratitude for being out of their hands. It is as well to know soon if I am seeing the truth or only dreaming the dreams of a girl."

"Yes. And if we learn that the Blade is alive and dangerous to the Rutari, there are other things we can do about him than send our men to fall off cliffs after him!" They both laughed.

"May I take Cheeky with me to the Idol?" Ellspa then asked. Cheeky gently took his hand off Moyla's shoulder. Now he would be sure to have thoughts he did not want *anyone* to hear.

"You think he will become your First Friend or at least tell you about the Blade?"

"Maybe. But—I would like to be kind to him. He does not deserve to be unhappy, no matter what his Master has done." What Ellspa was feeling told Cheeky that she was mostly telling the truth. She did hope to learn from him things about the Blade she did not know, but she also really wanted to make him happy.

Cheeky went over to Ellspa, *yeeeped* softly, and jumped up on her shoulder. "See," she said. "He understands me. In time, maybe he will be my First Friend. Now—can I take him with me to the Idol?"

"Yes."

Cheeky jumped down before there was any chance Ellspa could know why he was so happy and excited. He would learn where the Idol was and maybe even what it was. Then if the Master Blade was alive, and they ever met again, he would be able to tell Blade the things he most wanted to know! Then the Master Blade might forgive him for staying with Moyla.

However, that would be giving Blade something the Rutari did not want him to know. He would be making Ellspa unhappy after she tried to make him happy. The Wise One also might get angry with Ellspa, and punish her. Cheeky felt almost ashamed of himself for doing this to the woman. He knew it was a good thing to do for the Master Blade, but he very much wished the Master Blade was here so they could talk about it before he actually had to do it.

The Master Blade was not here, though. Cheeky would have to do what had to be done alone. For the first time he understood something about what the Master Blade felt all the times he had to do something like this alone.

Chapter 12

Richard Blade was still alive, but it wasn't because the Hungry Waters didn't live up to their name. As he'd once said, "I suppose I'm too stupid to know when I'm supposed to lie down and die. So I never do."

The spray threw off his judgment of the height of the cliff, so he hit the water before he was ready. He went deep, striking the bottom and swallowing a throatful of icy water before he started to rise. Then he shot to the surface like a cork, just in time for a wave to submerge him again. This bobbing up and down went on for quite a while, and if Blade hadn't been able to get a breath each time he surfaced he would probably have drowned.

Finally he reached a calmer part of the river. It turned out to be calmer only because the water boomed through a stretch of the canyon as straight as a pipe. Blade slammed against rocks several times, fortunately receiving only glancing blows. He wasn't hurt except for some bruises and loss of a certain amount of skin, but he was soon bleeding enough to notice. At least he didn't have to worry about the blood attracting sharks!

He'd just started to catch his breath when he went over a waterfall. It must have been a good thirty feet high, straight down into a pool so deep Blade didn't worry about hitting bottom. He shot down and down and down into it, until the light began to fade and he started won-

dering if he would get back to the surface before his breath
ran out. Or was he going to be sucked into an underwater
cave, just for variety?

Neither happened. His head popped into fresh air, and he
trod water until his lungs were back to normal. Then he
looked around. The pool was broad enough to slow down
the current. It was also far enough downstream from
where he'd jumped that the runners' path was nowhere in
sight. He still swam underwater most of the way to the
far bank, in case some of the runners who'd seen his accident left the path to look for him.

As soon as he felt bottom under his feet, he stood with
only his head out of the water, scanning the runners' side
of the river. The slope on his side was gentle, but as bare of
covering as a stripteaser at the end of her act. Anybody
who reached the other bank before Blade got over the
crest would see him standing out like a fly on a plate.

No sign of anyone, though. Blade swam the last few
yards to shore underwater, surfaced, took several deep
breaths, then charged out of the water. He didn't slow
down until he was over the crest of the slope, then looked
back at the opposite bank from the cover of a boulder.

He saw nobody, and he'd heard no shouts as he ran.
Blade checked his plastic harness and wrist bracers and
found himself grinning. Except for these bits of plastic he
was practically back to where he'd been in the early days
of the Project—alone and nearly naked, in a land full of
dangers, both human and natural.

This time, though, he knew most of the dangers,
including the Rutari and the Great Hunters. He knew
where he was going and roughly how far he had to go to get
there. He could even hope for a friendly reception when he
arrived. Considering how easily he'd survived so many
bare-arsed landings in entirely new Dimensions, there was
nothing to worry about now.

Or at least nothing to worry about as far as his own survival was concerned. Leaving Cheeky behind was another matter.

On the morning of the fourth day after he climbed out of the Hungry Waters, Blade was perched in the branches of one of the blue-leaved trees, watching the camp of what he assumed was an Uchendi hunting party. At least they weren't Rutari, and Blade hadn't heard of a third major tribe in this Dimension.

Five of the six hunters in the party had left at dawn, just after Blade settled into place. They'd left a hunter who was lying down with a bandaged leg, a small boy, and a good-looking if somewhat plump young woman. Blade could tell this because the Uchendi wore about as much as the Rutari. The girl wore a leather headband, sandals with throngs to the knee, and something like a set of dyed leather swimming trunks. This left a lot of well-rounded bronzed skin exposed to Blade's eyes.

The girl and the boy had just finished changing the bandage on the injured hunter's leg. The boy went off toward the bank of a nearby stream, carrying a sack. The girl built up the fire until a large clay pot was bubbling nicely, then started dropping the bones of yesterday's kill into the water. When the pot was full, she banked up the fire to keep it simmering, then picked up a bulging sack and went to feed the hunters' mounts.

The lizard-horses of the Uchendi had even longer legs than those of the Rutari; they reminded Blade more of spiders than of anything intended for riding by human beings. The girl had to reach up to feed them, but she seemed to have a way with them, cooing and clucking until they lowered their heads to nibble their food from her hand. Blade watched her move among the animals, admiring the way her black braids swung down her back and the springiness of her breasts—

A high-pitched scream came from the stream. The girl whirled and the hunter sat up in time to see the boy sprinting frantically back toward the camp. His eyes and mouth were wide with terror, and he had good reason for it. Behind him lumbered one of the Great Hunters. It didn't look like a full-grown specimen, but it was still taller than Blade and probably strong enough to strangle him one-handed. Devouring the three Uchendi would only whet his hearty appetite.

Blade swung down to a lower branch, then dropped to the ground on the far side of the tree and began searching for some large round stones. He had the only weapon that would give any of them a chance against the Great Hunter. It wasn't a very good chance, but the other choices were either running like a rabbit or watching the Great Hunter slaughter the Uchendi.

His hands closed on a stone of about the right size. It was heavier than he expected, but the Kaldakan plastic of his harness was strong enough to hurtle it. Blade started tugging one of the straps into shape. Between the heat of his body and the warmth of the morning it was almost too hard to shape. He was sweating by the time he had a use-able sling.

Meanwhile the Great Hunter hadn't noticed Blade or attacked the Uchendi. It lurched toward the lizard-horses. When they caught its scent and heard its cry, they went mad. Rearing and hissing, they broke their tethers and headed for the trees at a gallop. The Great Hunter lumbered after them for a few yards until the beast's slow wits discovered that it could never catch such swift prey. It turned back toward the three Uchendi.

By then Blade was ready with his improvised sling and four stones for it. He dropped the first one into place, stepped from behind the tree, then whirled the sling until it was a blur and let fly.

The stone whistled straight into the Great Hunter's chest, hard enough to make it grunt and stagger. A second one made it stop and look wildly around, trying to find this mysterious enemy. Blade picked up the third stone and took a more careful sight on the Great Hunter. He could bounce stones this size off the beast all day without doing damage, unless he hit it in the head.

As Blade whirled the sling for the third time, the injured hunter staggered to his feet. He was using his spear as a sort of crutch, and in his free hand held a short spiked club.

"Run, Eye of Crystal!"

"I will *not* leave you, River Over Stones!"

"Do you wish my company in the Sky Hunt?"

"If that is our fate—"

They nearly met their fate in the next moment. The Great Hunter charged, and River Over Stones raised his club. The movement drew the Great Hunter's eye. It turned, giving Blade a perfect shot. He released the sling, the stone flew free, and suddenly the Great Hunter was clawing at its throat, gasping, and trying to scream.

Then it was trying to breathe. A moment later it was down on the ground, writhing and coughing blood as shattered bones pierced flesh. The girl snatched the club from her companion's hand, dashed up to the Great Hunter, and brought the club down with both hands on its head. Its body arched in one final convulsion, then slumped limp in death.

Blade quickly reshaped the sling into a harness, then held his hands palms up and away from his body and stepped out into clear sight of the three Uchendi. They shifted their wide-eyed gaze from him to the dead Great Hunter, then back to him. River Over Stones raised his free hand in a vague salute, as if he didn't quite know what Blade was or how to greet him but knew he had to be polite to *anybody* who'd just saved his life.

Blade grinned. He knew he must look only a little less dangerous than the Great Hunter itself—gaunt, filthy, shaggy haired, and apparently able to slay Great Hunters by magic. He raised a hand in reply to River's gesture.

"Greetings. I am of the English. The name you may call me is Blade. Are you of the Uchendi?"

Eye of Crystal nodded. "You—the English? Where are they? Beyond the Rutari?" She sounded curious rather than suspicious.

"Yes," said Blade. "I entered Latan through lands of the Rutari. They asked me to do things unlawful for a warrior of the English, so I did not stay with them."

"The Rutari ask things unlawful for a mad dog!" snapped River.

That was a promising beginning to his stay among the Uchendi, Blade thought. He was just about to agree, when the boy cried out.

Four men were coming out of the nearest stretch of forest. They were carrying something like a wild boar covered with green scales on a litter improvised from four lances and a leather cloak. When they saw Blade, they dropped their kill and ran toward the campfire, swinging their lances. Before Blade or the Uchendi could take a step or say a word, the four hunters were upon them. Suddenly Blade found four sharp bronze points aimed at his stomach.

Chapter 13

Blade got into karate stance as fast as he could without making any sudden moves. From their headbands Blade could see that the four newcomers were clearly the rest of the Uchendi hunting party returning with their kill; they should be friendly after they heard what Blade had done.

Crystal spoke sharply. "Put down your weapons. This is the warrior Blade of the English. He slew a *shpuga* with a magical English weapon and saved us."

The lance points wavered, but the four men didn't move. Their eyes shifted to River Over Stones. "Is this true?" one said.

River looked from Blade to Crystal, then nodded slowly. "We might not be alive without the magic of the English." Then his expression changed subtly, into something Blade didn't quite understand but knew he didn't like. The man no longer looked quite so friendly. "But I do not know if there is a price to be paid for being saved by English magic. Is your magic unclean, Blade?"

Blade knew he had to weigh his words as carefully as he'd done before the Wise One. This man might not be telepathic, but he was playing some game. "That is not a word used among the English, River Over Stones. So I can swear no oath about my magic that would mean anything. Not until I know more of the magic of the Uchendi."

"The Rutari taught you nothing about it?" said Crystal.

Blade laughed harshly. "They *told* me much. They are also your mortal enemies, so why should I believe anything they told me?"

Everyone except River Over Stones laughed at this. The hunter frowned. "Then—we may have been saved by unclean magic. I would rather have died quickly, by the *shpuga*."

"I would rather not have died at all," said Crystal. "And we did not."

"Spoken like a woman," said River Over Stones. Crystal glared at him, and the lance points rose again. Blade knew that if River so much as blinked an eye, he was going to be the first one down. Blade didn't plan to kill anybody, but he had the feeling the conversation would go a lot better with fewer lances pointed at his stomach.

Before the tension could spark a fight, a fifth hunter came out of the trees, took one look at the camp, then broke into a run. As he reached them, the four hunters lowered their lance points. They looked relieved. River Over Stones looked sullenly at the ground.

"Wait until you are healed before you give orders, if you cannot wait until I am dead," said the new arrival coldly.

"Only Crystal was here beside me," said River. "Should I let a woman command, Father?"

"Yes, if she has more sense than you," said the new hunter. Blade now saw deep lines in his face, gray in his hair, and a long scar down one arm. "Eye of Crystal, this man is angry, is he not?" he said, looking at Blade.

"Yes, and with good reason." Crystal told the story of Blade's arrival and the battle against the Great Hunter—or *shpuga*. The other hunters told of what happened after they arrived. By the time everyone was finished, River Over Stones looked as if he would like to sink into the ground or strangle Blade, and didn't know which.

The older hunter, whose name was Winter Owl, listened

in silence, then paced up and down for a moment before replying. "The Spirit Voice speaks to Eye of Crystal strongly, so that she knows this man is angry. It does not speak to her as strongly as it does to her father: He Who Guards the Voice. Only he can hear what lies within this warrior, Blade of the English, and know if his magic is clean. Shall we bring Blade before He Who Guards the Voice, or shall we slay him as River over Stones thinks best?"

Crystal closed her eyes suddenly. "Mother's brother Winter Owl, you have made Blade even more angry than he was."

Blade looked sharply at the girl. Was she reading his mind without the aid of the *kerush*, or just bluffing to help him? Certainly she was telling the truth. He decided to use that fact.

"Yes, I am angry," said Blade. He crossed his arms on his chest. "Do the Uchendi have neither honor nor sense? If so, I will neither appear before He Who Guards the Voice nor stand here and be slain. I will find my friends among the *shpugas*, who seem to be more like men than the Uchendi! Winter Owl, you appear wiser than others here. What do you wish? And let your tongue move swiftly, before my feet do so."

This at least got Blade an explanation of what was involved here. The Uchendi couldn't be sure whether the unknown magic Blade used against the *shpuga* was unclean and wouldn't also curse the people he'd saved. A wizard's curse, however, died when the wizard himself did. So it might be wise to kill him, just on the chance that he'd done something bad to River Over Stones, Eye of Crystal, and the boy by saving their lives.

On the other hand, his magic might be perfectly clean. But Crystal couldn't be sure, and she was the most powerful telepath among the band of hunters. They could take Blade to her father, He Who Guards the Voice, who was the chief shaman of the Uchendi, and have him examine

Blade. But that would mean keeping company with a possibly dangerous wizard for several days, and who could say
what curses he might lay on those around him in that
time?

After Winter Owl's explanation came a long argument
among the six hunters. If sadistic cruelty was the Rutari
tribal vice, debate seemed to be the Uchendi one.

While all the party were equal, obviously Eye of Crystal
and her uncle, Winter Owl, were a little more equal than
the rest and they saved Blade from being put to death for
possible unclean magic. Also, two of the hunters pointed
out that, wizard or not, Blade looked like a good man to
help them catch their strayed mounts. The longer they
argued about him, the more likely their mounts would
wander too far to be caught. Did River Over Stones want
to walk all the way home with his injured leg, or did he
hope the wizard could fly him through the air?

Blade never got a clear idea of what River Over Stones
wanted, except possibly that Richard Blade should disappear in a puff of smoke. He did see the man sullenly agree
to spare Blade, if Blade would perform no more magic until
He Who Guards the Voice had examined him.

"This I swear," said Blade, "by the earth and the
blood, the sky and the fire, by my manhood and my hope of
sons—unless another *shpuga* comes against me, and there
is no other way to protect us from it."

That satisfied everyone, and Blade was paired up with
Winter Owl when the party scattered to track their
straying mounts.

It took the rest of the day to track down the *ezinti*, as
the Uchendi called the lizard-horses. It took two more
days to ride downriver to the settled land of the Uchendi,
and two more to reach He Who Guards the Voice.

By then Blade was pretty sure he'd made the right deci-
sion in coming to the Uchendi—if they would let him stay
among them. They talked too much and they were just as

superstitious in their own way as the Rutari, but otherwise it was easy to get along with them.

They stopped at the first village they came to. The *ezinti* badly needed fat meat by this time; they'd been living off grass and the leavings of the hunters so long that the short rations were beginning to take their toll.

Winter Owl bought half a dozen of the villager's pigs, partly with some of the hides of his party's kills and partly with strings of green-dyed nutshells. There were several kinds of nutshells used as money among the Uchendi, as well as disks of polished stone strung on thongs and bronze chisels. In return for beer for the whole party, Winter Owl had Eye of Crystal visit an old woman of the village, who was sick and in continuous pain.

Blade would gladly have watched Crystal at her healing work. However, River Over Stones got to the village chief before Winter Owl did, and warned him about Blade. Fearful of English magic, the chief kept Blade in a hut on the far side of the village.

Blade met Crystal when she'd finished with the old woman. She was wandering outside his hut, her hair hung in tangled strings, and her eyes not focusing on anything until she practically stumbled into Blade's arms. She didn't speak clearly until she'd gulped down a skinful of beer.

"She will die," Crystal said. "I cannot save her. I cannot even find the courage to tell her husband the truth. Is it my Voice that is weak, or me?" She gulped more beer. "Can the magic of the English save a woman, when a part of her body goes mad and starts eating the other parts?"

Cancer, Blade thought. Aloud, he said, "We have many magics, some stronger than others. Sometimes we can fight a person's body going mad, or if necessary, cut off the mad part. Sometimes, for all our magic, we can do nothing but try to find the courage to tell the person he is going to die."

"But you are not helpless against the madness? You can

at least, like us, teach the person how to think so that he will not feel the pain?''

''That wisdom we do not have. At least not many of us.'' Blade remembered tales of yoga adepts and fire-walkers, who seemed to be able to fight pain entirely by mental control. Could the Uchendi telepaths not only do this but teach it? If Blade had been a hunting animal, his ears would have been pricking up.

Eye of Crystal, however, was past doing or teaching anything. The beer was hitting her, and she slumped into Blade's arms, head against his chest and hair trailing over his shoulder. He held her quietly, very conscious of the magnificent breasts against his bare skin. He was even more conscious that the last thing on her mind would be sex. What she needed now was some rest and peace of mind.

He held her until she stopped mumbling, then brought her in his hut and laid her down on the furs and stripped off her clothes. His heavy-boned hands with the long fingers, which could break a man's neck at one blow, now became precision instruments, working up and down Crystal's bare body, unknotting tension-twisted muscles, working a lit-tle magic of Blade's own.

Crystal was sound asleep by the time Blade finished. Blade became aware that someone was standing silhou-etted against the twilight at the door of the hut. It was River Over Stones, and nobody could have mistaken his expression.

''You have touched her with your magic—?''

''I touched her with English healing magic, because she needed healing too. Nothing more, nothing less. If you say to anyone else that I have done more, I will call you a liar.''

''I cannot challenge a wizard. That is a vile trick, Blade!''

''I will need no magic to tear you into small pieces and use you for *shpuga* bait. Your mouth is the only strong part of your body, and I think Eye of Crystal knows it. Do not make me show all the Uchendi what you are.''

Blade had risen to his feet while speaking, and in the dim light of the hut he must have looked as formidable as a *shpuga*. River Over Stones grunted something Blade doubted was a compliment, then backed away.

Blade shrugged. He'd made an open enemy of someone who would never have been a friend anyway. That wasn't losing much. River Over Stones would keep his mouth shut, unless Crystal or Winter Owl brought up the matter. God knows what Uchendi law he might have violated by giving Crystal the massage she so obviously needed!

Chapter 14

Eye of Crystal sang as the hunting party rode the last mile to the main village of the Uchendi. She usually sang when she was feeling happy, and once she'd recovered from treating the cancer-stricken old woman she seemed to be happy most of the time.

Blade didn't want her to be unhappy. He was glad that his massage and other gestures of friendship helped Crystal shake off the memories of her helplessness. He still wished that she would find some other way of showing her happiness than by singing. Eye of Crystal was intelligent, brave, good-looking, and Blade suspected she would be good in bed. But she could not carry a tune with a pair of tongs, and was always off-key.

However, River Over Stones proclaimed her singing sweeter than a bird's. Blade couldn't entirely disagree. Eye of Crystal sounded better than a crow, a vulture, or most seagulls.

Blade couldn't decide if River Over Stones really expected Crystal to be taken in by such gross flattery. If he did, he was crazy, or at least didn't know the woman he was courting. No wonder she was barely polite to him, and sometimes not polite at all. Blade knew that if River Over Stones hadn't been the adopted "war-son" of her uncle Winter Owl, she would not have even been polite.

"River Over Stone is in a strange place," she told him

once. "He is no blood-kin, so if he is purified it is lawful for him to wed me. So he courts with all seriousness. Yet he is law-kin, so that an open quarrel between us would divide a family. This is something no wise man can wish, my father and uncle least of all."

"Does he have so many enemies, then?" No harm in trying to get a little more information about what he might be riding into.

"Do you know so little of life among kin, then? Were you an orphan?"

"No."

"Then I think you are trying to learn what I would not be wise to tell you now, before we know how you may use the knowledge."

"You seem to trust me as little as River Over Stones does."

"I will even endure that insult, Blade. I do not dislike you and I am not your enemy. Nor do I think my father will be either, when he has spoken to you as the law says he must. But until that time, who can say for sure whether you are a good man or what River Over Stones thinks you are? That we may be friends, please do not again seek to know what you may not."

"On the blood of my kills and trueness of my eye, I swear I will not." No one could doubt Blade's right to swear on those. He did *not* like having good-looking women angry at him, particularly if they were also as intelligent as Eye of Crystal.

If only she could learn to sing!

The hunters rode for miles through cultivated fields before they reached the village. The village itself was almost a town, stretching for a quarter of a mile along the bank of the River of Life. They even had a waterwheel at the upstream end of the village, pumping water into a tank of stone and clay. From there the women hauled buckets of water to their homes.

Blade also noticed that the stables for the *ezintis*, the tanners and smiths and slaughterhouses, and what smelled like public toilets were all at the downstream end of the village. These people seemed to have grasped the basics of sanitation. Blade's opinion of the Uchenti went up another notch.

The village was completely surrounded by a ten-foot wall of logs with thorny bushes tied to the top. At the foot of the wall was an equally deep ditch, crossed by four bridges to guarded gates. Pointed stakes jutted upward from the bottom of the ditch. Blade hoped all this fortification was just against *shpugas*, but it looked too strong and too new. In fact, one of the gateways was still under construction.

The Uchendi were preparing for war—a war in which they expected to have to fight the Rutari to the last ditch. A war in which Richard Blade was also sure to be involved, if it took place while he was still in this Dimension.

Blade wondered if he'd jumped out of the frying pan into the fire. He also hoped that Crystal's father and uncle would be up to the job of leading their people in a desperate battle. Blade knew he was good, but on the whole he wasn't quite sure he was up to the job of playing Winston Churchill to the Uchendi. Assuming, of course, they would let him try.

Blade reined his *ezinti* to a stop as the nearest gate of the village opened and spewed out people. There were no more than fifty, but they were shouting and laughing loud enough for two hundred. His beast began to balk and jitter, and Blade had to concentrate on keeping it under control or at least keeping his seat. He was *not* going to spoil his first appearance at the capital of the Uchendi by falling on his arse.

It was some slight consolation to Blade that Winter Owl was having just as much trouble not going head over heels. There was a middle-aged woman clinging to his leg with one hand and pounding his thigh with the other, to emphasize her points. Winter Owl looked down at her, with a long-suffering smile on his face.

"Mother!" Crystal's voice cut through the din. "I know you're glad to see us home. Will you be so glad to see your brother trampled flat as scraped *ezinti* hide?"

"Hold your tongue, Eye of Crystal," said the woman, but there was laughter in her voice. "When this—mighty warrior was a small naked boy, yes, there were many times I hoped the *ezintis* would do dreadful things to him. Alas, they never heard my prayers."

"Since neither the *shpugas* nor the Uchendi seem to have done that work either, what could the *ezintis* have possibly done?" said Winter Owl. "Would you have had the *ezintis* perish trying to rid you of me, so that the hunters could not ride and the Uchendi would go hungry for meat? Really, Kyarta my sister, you have no sense when you think of how to rid yourself of me!"

Obviously this was an old game between them, one everybody in the village was used to. Blade saw broad grins all around him as the exchange of insults and accusations grew wider. Then suddenly everyone fell silent, as if they'd been struck mute. Winter Owl's mount reared once more, then even it was calm.

A man was walking toward the crowd. Blade knew without being told that this was Crystal's father, He Who Guards the Voice, and thought to himself that he hoped the man had a shorter name! Like his daughter, he was short and squarely built, but without her pleasing roundness. His scarred but unwrinkled brown skin was stretched tightly over what were obviously still rock-hard muscles. He wore only a loinguard of *ezinti* hide and a necklace of copper disks; his nearly bald scalp was tattooed in complex swirling patterns of green and yellow.

He was smiling as he approached, but in spite of the smile he looked as if he'd be every bit as shrewd and formidable an enemy or friend as the Wise One.

Blade dismounted and advanced to meet the man who was also called Guardian.

"I am Blade, a warrior of England. I came into Latan in the lands of the Rutari, but they asked of me things that are unlawful for me. So I came away from them, and—"

"Guardian! He is a wizard who slew a *shpuga* by unclean magic!" No need to ask if that was River Over Stones running on as usual.

"By magic that *may* be unclean," said Eye of Crystal, "but we don't know—"

"He used it on the *shpuga* where she and I were present!" shouted River. "Who can be sure if her tongue is her own?"

"If you were there, then the same can be said of your tongue!" snapped Crystal. "As well as all the other things that can be said of it," she added spitefully.

Blade mentally counted to ten. *Here we go again with the Uchendi national sport of arguing.* River's outburst had done its dirty work, too, even though Crystal now seemed to be holding her own. People were backing away from Blade, pointing and whispering. Nobody was smiling now, and some of the looks turned toward Blade were a long way from friendly.

One of these days I am going to strangle River Over Stones with my bare hands and claim I was just getting rid of a public nuisance, thought Blade. He really didn't care for the idea of having somebody like that at his back, no matter what the Guardian might say.

First things first, again. Get the Guardian on your side, then stuff something in River's big mouth.

Blade waited until River and Crystal seemed to run out of breath. So did the Guardian. Then, before anyone else could join in, Blade stepped close to the Guardian and gave him a military salute.

"By this sign of the warriors of England, I submit myself to your judgment of the lawfulness of my magic. Your name is honored among the Uchendi for your knowledge of the Spirit world and your great sense of judgment. Therefore I do not fear receiving other than justice at your hands."

The Guardian grinned, showing yellow but even teeth. "A very pretty speech, Blade of England. So pretty that I am almost tempted to refuse to give you judgment, lest my people think you flattered me into it."

"Father—" began Crystal.

"Be silent!" shouted River. "You speak when the Guardian listens to another. The law—"

"IS BETTER KNOWN TO ME THAN TO EITHER OF YOU!" bellowed the Guardian, in a voice that made everyone around him jump. Blade's ears rang, and two men working on the gateway were so startled they fell into the ditch.

"Very good," said the Guardian, "now that my ears are no longer being beaten by words heavier than a smith's hammer and not nearly as useful . . . River Over Stones, be silent now or face being made silent for a longer time." The young warrior glared but held his tongue. "Daughter, you did not tell me that this man Blade had come for judgment."

"I—I—"

"You were too busy arguing with River Over Stones. I forgive you for shaming my teaching, just this once. The next time you forget how I taught you to always tell all things that need to be known, I shall not be so gentle."

The Guardian turned back to Blade. "You have indeed come for judgment of your magic? All your magic ways?"

"I do not know all the ways of magic among the Uchendi," said Blade. "Certainly I will submit to your judgment in all ways known among the English. The rest may be judged by the Spirits, if judgment is needed." He smiled. "I know I will receive a wiser judgment here than they sought to give me among the Rutari."

That went over well, judging from the new grins, and it was also perfectly true—at least if Blade was judged by

Crystal's father. But if River Over Stones had been giving the judgment . . .

"May the Spirits desert us if this is not so," said Crystal, and her father nodded.

"Now, Blade, I think it best we go to my house—"

"Open judgment, open judgment, open judgment!" screamed River Over Stones. Several people took up the cry. Crystal looked ready to castrate her suitor, and the Guardian was frowning.

"If there is a call for the judgment to be reached with others present, I must submit to it," he said. "It seems to me this is not wise with unknown magic, but it is the law."

"My magic may not be lawful by the ways of the Uchendi," said Blade. "But if my oath means anything, I give it here, that I will use no magic in the judgment and no man witnessing it need fear me. Is that enough?"

"More than enough," said the Guardian, in a voice daring River to disagree. The young man gritted his teeth, then also nodded.

Blade let the Guardian and Crystal lead him away from the village, toward a patch of open ground just short of the fields. He couldn't really say that being probed telepathically—which is what the judgment consisted of—and maybe being rendered helpless in the presence of at least fifty possible enemies was his favorite way to spend a morning.

On the other hand, if he passed the judgment in the eyes of all the witnesses, he would be sure of his acceptance among the Uchendi. There was always a moment when you had to stop running, and this looked like a good moment to at least try.

Chapter 15

Blade didn't know what to expect after they reached the open ground. He settled for breathing slowly and deeply, to get his mind and body under as much control as he could.

He also kept a watchful eye open for an escape route. He did want to stop his running here if he could, but wouldn't stop if the Uchendi were setting him up for murder. The circle of would-be witnesses around the testing area grew steadily thicker, but at least only a few of them were armed. Children kept wandering too far forward and being hauled back by their parents.

The Guardian's wife Kyarta also wanted to get a good look at Blade, but Eye of Crystal stopped her. The two women started another half-serious argument, too far from Blade for him to hear more than one word in three. Winter Owl did not intervene—he was too busy placing the handful of armed men at precise intervals around the circle of witnesses. River Over Stones also kept his mouth shut for once. Probably he expected Blade's testing to prove that he'd been right all along about the Englishman's having evil magic.

While all this was going on, the Guardian was standing in the center of the bare ground, his feet slightly apart, his arms crossed on his chest, and his eyes on the ground. It was impossible to tell whether he was hypnotizing himself, communing with the Spirits, or simply trying to fight off boredom.

Finally the Guardian raised his head.

"Blade, come here." He might have been addressing a puppy who'd made a mess on the floor. Blade swallowed his resentment at the tone, assuming it was part of the ritual, and obeyed the command.

"Blade, stop right there." Blade did so, about six feet from the Guardian.

"Is it the custom among the English to use the Seed of Wisdom?"

"By this, do you mean what the—your enemies—call the *kerush*?"

"That is their unlawful name for the sacred seed, yes. You are forgiven for using that name in this place—once."

"I will have no need to call it by other than its lawful name now that I know that name."

"You certainly have *some* wisdom. So: do you use the Seed of Wisdom in English magic?"

"No. But I did use it when I was among your enemies. It made it easier for them to learn about my magic. It also made it easier for me to learn how unlawful their wishes were for me. I do not know if your magic is like your enemies' magic, or if you and I will also need the Seed of Wisdom. And that is not seeking to gain knowledge I must not have. It is just the wisdom of knowing that I do not know everything."

Blade hoped this effort at tact would pay off. He only knew as much about Uchendi telepathy as the Rutari had told him, which wasn't much. It certainly didn't include what form of the *kerush* the Uchendi used, and he didn't like the idea of taking unknown quantities of drugs even among a people who'd treated him decently.

In fact, he didn't even know if he would *be* telepathic without either Cheeky or the *kerush*. But he wasn't going to hint at that possibility, not with someone as shrewd as the Guardian.

There was a long silence. It seemed to Blade that this trip to Dimension X was full of long silences, while he or somebody else decided what to do next. He'd read science fiction stories in which telepathy solved all human problems. All his experience with telepathy so far suggested that it caused more problems than it solved. The only thing he'd really gained from telepathy was Cheeky—and then he'd lost the feather-monkey to a case of the hots!

Blade's eyes roamed around the circle of witnesses. River Over Stones was looking nakedly triumphant. Winter Owl's face was unreadable, but his eyes moved back and forth, from the Guardian to Blade. Eye of Crystal was frowning, but this might be her mother's fault. Kyarta looked ready to shout advice to her husband.

Then the Guardian smiled. Blade didn't need to hear River Over Stones's snarled obscenity to know that was a good sign. "You do indeed show much wisdom. Also a kind of courage not common in a warrior: the courage to admit a weakness."

"If you wish to kill me, Guardian, you can do so whether you know my weaknesses or not. If you do not wish to kill me, then knowing my weaknesses will do me no harm. Indeed, it may keep you from killing me by chance. I do not think you would be happy to do that."

"I would not. But let us leave the contest of praise until after I have tested you. For now, I will say that we boil the Seed of Wisdom with water and the juices of fruit. Then we drink it. Does this seem to make it dangerous for you?"

"It does not."

"Good. Then it is my advice that you drink it. If you have survived the *kerush-magor* of our enemies, our Sweet Wisdom can do you no harm. Also, it will make your testing easier."

"Do you wish to make my testing so much easier, that I might succeed where I ought to have failed? Is that wise for you and the Uchendi?"

"As you say, Blade of the English, if I want to kill you I can do so easily. And I assure you that if you fail the testing I will very probably wish to kill you. By making the testing easy I mean only that it will take less strength from either of us. I should guard my strength for other tasks, you also if you do succeed."

That made sense, and Blade said so, then added, "Bring me the Sweet Wisdom, and I shall drink it."

The Guardian clapped his hands, and Eye of Crystal herself ran out, carrying a gourd closed with a gilded-leather stopper on a loop of thin copper wire.

The Sweet Wisdom fizzed like a carbonated beverage; the Uchendi must have mixed it with gasified water from a natural spring. The fruit juice was purple and sweet without being overpowering, like a cross between an apple and a peach. Blade knew that the slight bitterness of the *kerush* would be lost under the sweetness, so he didn't waste time trying to guess the dosage. He simply drank the gourd empty, then set it down.

"You should sit down, Blade," said the Guardian, pointing at the ground.

Blade started to shake his head, then found his knees quivering slightly. He quickly obeyed the Guardian so none of the watchers would suspect him of being afraid.

Then suddenly the world twisted around him, so much like it did during a Transition that he half expected to see the booth surrounding him. Instead the circle of Uchendi spectators seemed to widen enormously, until they were only a dark fringe of barely human figures around a vast empty expanse of bare earth.

At the same time Blade felt as if his head were sitting on a sheet of glass, entirely separate from his body but still alive. He could see his body down there below the glass, but he couldn't make it do anything or feel any sensation from it. He was a disembodied brain attached to just enough sense organs to remind him that there *was* something outside his brain.

So he wasn't surprised to hear the Guardian's voice as if it was spoken both in his mind and in his ears.

("Welcome to the Sphere of Wisdom, Blade.")

("It is for you to say if I am welcome or not, He Who Guards the Voice.")

("You are more welcome because you have come here swiftly. And yes, that is a good sign for your judgment, and yes again, I can see even the beginning of a thought and from that beginning read the whole.")

("I can see why you were sure you could kill me easily.")

("Very surely, Blade. Without much effort, I could stop your heart. With a little more effort, I could make you tear your flesh from your bones with your own hands. I have not punished anyone that way in my whole life, but He Who Guards the Voice before me did it three times and died of old age. . . . And tell me, Blade, who is Lord—Lay-tun—and why should he wish to know me?")

("Lord Leighton was my teacher. He is a great teacher among the English, and would give much to learn the Wisdom and the Voice of the Uchendi.")

("From your mind I understand that he is an old man. Did he begin to learn the Voice and the Wisdom when he was six years old, as I did?")

("He did not.")

("Do you English know so little of the Voice and the Wisdom that you do not teach it to your children?")

("There are many among the English who use these things for evil purposes. So it is unlawful for all but warriors such as myself to learn.")

("That seems to me like burning down the village to kill the rats in one hut. Of course the Voice and the Wisdom are ill used, if they are not properly taught. Few who are not taught before they are men and women will ever learn properly!")

The mental equivalent of a shrug and then: ("This Lay-tun seems to be a very great teacher indeed, so I would like to meet him, but your mind also tells me that Lay-tun is far away. A man that old might not survive such a long journey. He cannot come here, and I cannot leave my people in their time of need? . . . Yes, I will tell you what that need is, when you have passed your testing.'')

(''Then perhaps it will be best for all the Uchendi if you go on with the testing.'')

(''Most surely, Blade. But I must say that you have done much to pass it already. You entered the Sphere of Wisdom quickly, showed no fear at meeting me there, and did not seek in vain to hide your thoughts. Nor do you have the aura that any man who works unclean magic would have when he has reached your age. Yet I must go deeper into your mind to finish the testing.'')

(''Then do so.'')

(''Breathe quickly and deeply until you become dizzy. Then empty your mind of all thoughts, and fear nothing.'')

Blade laughed. When he'd hyperventilated enough, his mind would be empty of all thoughts, whether he wanted it to be or not. He figured, it would do him no harm—he was already at the Guardian's mercy, and if death did come now it would most likely be quick.

He raised his arms and took the first deep breath, then the second, then the third, and after that a steady rhythm. . . .

Darkness and a great shape looming over him, a fanged head on a long neck and great wings spreading into the shadows. Blade was naked and holding a curiously modern rifle, aimed at the shape. Then the shape blazed orange flame, and he smelled the swamp-stench of methane. He raised the rifle to his shoulder and took aim, knowing where he was.

The Guardian was making him go way back into his mind to relive his trips to other Dimensions. Now he was in the Dimension of the strange other-England called Englor, facing a biologically-engineered dragon sent against Englor by the Red Flames of Russland. Behind him was an inn and Rylla, the Russland scientist who'd helped develop the dragons before she defected. If he didn't find the dragon's vulnerable spots before it set the inn on fire . . .

A steel corridor stretching ahead and behind as far as he could see. Other corridors branching off on either side. He was running, with something like a laser in his hand. Around him were other men with lasers, also running, also wearing uniformlike jumpsuits.

He was aboard the *Avenger,* the giant starship built by Earth's mad dictator Loyun Chard. He and his comrades, aided by a woman named Riyannah from a distant world, were going to destroy the ship to keep Chard from taking death and destruction to the distant stars. . . .

Mist swirling, and in the background vast colored cylinders soaring up toward the sky, so tall their tops seemed to be lost in the mist or the clouds. Hard-packed gravel underfoot, and silence everywhere.

He was standing among the Towers of Melnon, on the ground where they'd fought out their ritualized but deadly combats until Blade took a hand. . . .

The deck of a ship heaving under his feet, the smell of salt air, and the creak of rigging or perhaps oars. Somewhere a rough voice was shouting orders.

He couldn't tell where he was—there'd been so many ships and so many seas in so many Dimensions, and deadly battles in all of them. . . .

A vast blue-lit chamber, with pulsing walls that seemed to be made of living flesh. At the far end a delicate latticework of crystal rods and shining wires, and a terrible *presence.* Blade had no trouble in recognizing the Ngaa, the Dimension X monster the experimental KALI capsule had unleashed on Home Dimension.

He also had no trouble recognizing the woman in the white nurse's uniform lying on the floor between him and the Ngaa: Zoé Cornwall. His first and truest love, and now he suspected likely to be his last. Snatched into this

Dimension of horror because in her love for him she'd battled for his sanity against the Ngaa that had driven him mad.

He ran forward and lifted her in his arms. He could tell that she recognized him. He could also tell that she was dying, that the Ngaa was killing her—

And that this time he would see her death from *inside her own mind*.

No.

("No! I will not let you put me through this. I refuse. THERE ARE SOME THINGS YOU CANNOT MAKE ME DO AND THIS IS ONE OF THEM. GET OUT OF MY MIND, YOU FILTHY BARBARIAN GHOUL!")

The sensation of Zoé in his arms and her mind linked to his vanished in a blur of light so dazzling that Blade cried out from the pain in his eyes. Thunder cracked in his head, then rumbled away into silence.

He felt himself weightless, as if he were in space or falling from a great height. All around him was blue, but somehow it was a saner, more healthy blue than the nightmare light of the Ngaa's chamber of death.

The Guardian was falling beside him, his arms outstretched, looking helpless and even frightened for the first time. It was hard to judge distances in this blueness, but the shaman seemed close enough to reach out and touch.

A great pulsing golden bar was growing rapidly below them. Blade somehow knew that he would fall across the bar and be saved. If he reached out a hand and gripped the Guardian, the man would also be saved. If he let the Guardian fall past the bar, however . . .

The bar slammed Blade in the stomach so hard all the wind *whooossshed* out of him. It was a terrifyingly strong physical sensation to have in this world he'd been told was a thing of the mind. It also confirmed his judgment, that he should reach out and catch the Guardian.

Blade balanced himself across the bar so that he could

use both hands to reach out. The steel-hard muscles of his arms rippled under the skin as he pulled the Guardian to a stop in midair, then started hauling him in like a gaffed fish. The man's eyes were blank and staring. Blade couldn't help wondering if he'd been too late, if he was hauling in a dead man—

Then he was hauling an unconscious man toward him across the bare earth of the testing place, with a two-handed grip on the man's left wrist. Blade hastily let go. His hands were strong enough to break the shaman's older and smaller bones if he wasn't careful! The arm flopped limply to the ground. . . . Blade heard a hiss of indrawn breath and an angry muttering all around him.

He looked up. Everyone who wasn't looking at the unconscious Guardian was looking at him, and he didn't like most of the looks. He wasn't sure what he'd done to the Guardian, though he was sure it was an accident. That obviously didn't matter to the circle of witnesses. Blade had never seen anything that looked quite so much like the beginning of a lynch mob.

He wouldn't kill Eye of Crystal or her mother, he decided. He would try not to kill Winter Owl if he could avoid it. The Uchendi would need him if the Guardian was dead or mindless. Anyone else who got in his way had better look out.

Blade bent over the Guardian's wrist and felt for a pulse. One was there, and it was steady but also weak enough to worry Blade. He drew the man toward him, ready to start mouth-to-mouth respiration or even cardiopulmonary resuscitation if he had to.

A howl of rage came from the crowd.

"He works further magic," shouted someone. "Kill him now."

Blade stood up, ready to move fast, but just then a hysterical screech from a woman cut through the crowd noises. It might have launched everybody forward to tear Blade to pieces. Instead it stopped everyone who'd started moving, as if they'd stepped into concrete. It was the Guardian's wife Kyarta. She went on screaming as Eye of Crystal tried to hold her up, calm her down, and get her to drink some water all at once.

Before anybody else could do anything wise or foolish, the Guardian groaned and sat up. He looked to Blade like a man suffering from a crashing hangover. However, he was definitely alive and conscious, and possibly even of sound mind. About the sound body, Blade wasn't going to take any bets now.

Blade knelt again, which accomplished two things. It looked like a gesture of respect, and he and the Guardian could talk without strain or the risk of anyone overhearing them.

"I am sorry if I have done you harm," Blade whispered. "But what you asked of me—I would rather die than give it, no matter to whom."

The Guardian blinked and seemed to be able to focus on Blade for the first time. "You—die? I was far closer to death than you could have been."

"That was not my wish."

"I know. But—I have never been hurled out of a man's mind like that before. I was doomed but for your help."

"If I have passed my testing—"

"Oh you have, you have," the Guardian said almost irritably. "You have done so well I think it may have been a waste of my time to test you at all."

"I thank you," said Blade. "Now, if I have passed my testing, will you teach me as much about the Wisdom and the Voice as you think I can learn? Clearly you will not be the only man I can put in danger, if I have this kind of strength in my mind."

Then he looked around the circle and added quickly, "But first, could you tell these people that I have passed the test and you are not hurt? Otherwise I fear I shall not live long enough to be taught anything, or else have to kill some of your people to keep them from killing me."

The Guardian managed to laugh. "Certainly, Blade of the English. If you will help me to stand . . ."

Blade pulled the Guardian to his feet and then held him with a hand under one arm as he spoke to the crowd. "Put down your weapons and set aside your anger," he began. He had to repeat himself twice before anyone heard him, and twice more before people started obeying. Then he had to be quiet until he'd caught his breath.

"Blade of the English has passed his testing. He is a good man, with a great power, but his people did not teach him how to use it to the fullest."

"He used that power against *you!*" shouted River Over Stones. "How can he be within the law?" Mutters of agreement.

"Do you know the law better than I? Is it the custom that a barely fledged warrior shall dispute He Who Guards the Voice?" That silenced River Over Stones, but not the muttering.

"Blade is a mighty warrior. His strength and his skill and his heart are all good, though he does not know all that he ought to know about using them. He has traveled far, fought in many lands, and used strange and magical weapons. I have seen them, and I have also seen that he always used them lawfully, against unlawful enemies."

"Then why did he fight you?" said someone. He didn't sound angry now, just curious. That was a considerable improvement.

The Guardian whispered, "Blade, I must tell the tale of your—dying woman—before they will understand. May I?" Blade nodded.

"The last memory I reached was the death of the woman he loved most, at the hands of a great and evil magician." Blade supposed that was as good a description of the Ngaa as any other these people would understand. "He would not live through her death again, so he drove me from his mind. He did not wish me harm, only that I should not know something that indeed I did not need to know, because it was very painful for him to think of it.''

The Guardian seemed to glare at each person in the circle of witnesses in turn. ''Who here has not lost one they loved? And who here would care to live through the moment of that death again? If there is one among you who would not fear to do that, he may speak against Blade. Everyone else will keep silent or face my anger.''

The silence was agreeably long. Blade reflected again on how the Guardian could control a crowd. He knew that if the shaman had spoken against him, the people would have swarmed over him and torn him to pieces with their bare hands no matter how many he killed. When it came to being either a good friend or a deadly enemy, He Who Guards the Voice of the Uchendi made the Wise One of the Rutari look like a child.

The Guardian turned toward Blade. ''It seems our day's work is done. I thank you for your help. As for teaching you—may we speak of that another day? I am not against the idea. But I am more in favor of food, sleep, and beer now. Travel into the Sphere of Wisdom can be as hard as war. . . .''

If Blade hadn't known before that telepathy could be hard work, he knew now. He wasn't sleepy, but he very much wanted to sit down. Sweat was streaming off him, and his mouth felt like a lump of charcoal. Sitting down and letting Eye of Crystal serve him hot food and cool beer did seem the best way to spend the rest of the day.

''And of course, my daughter will be glad to honor you by serving you,'' said the Guardian.

Blade was fairly sure he hadn't felt any telepathic contact from the Guardian just then—but then, did a loving, observant father need telepathy to know when his daughter was attracted to a man?

Chapter 16

"More beer?" said Eye of Crystal.

Blade held up his empty wooden cup and contemplated it by the light of the fire in his hut. Good. He saw only one cup. It was too early in the evening for him to be so drunk that he was seeing two cups, particularly since he'd only been drinking beer.

However, he was in a mood to celebrate. "Do you have anything stronger?"

"Stronger? How?"

"More—more of what there is in beer to make you—"

"Piss a lot?"

Blade laughed. "That wasn't quite what I had in mind." He tried to explain alcohol, then wine and distilled beverages. Unlike the Rutari, the Uchendi apparently hadn't invented distilling.

"There is winter ale," said Eye of Crystal dubiously. "It is stronger than summer ale, in the way that you talk about. Are you stronger than it?"

"I am stronger than anything men can make to drink," said Blade with mock bravado. Except some really Godawful cheap Turkish raki he and a friend and fellow agent (now dead) had drunk once, to celebrate a minor victory. Come to think of it, he still wasn't quite sure the stuff hadn't been poisoned. Probably not by the Russians, though—more likely by the brothel-keeper they'd put out

119

of business in the process of uncovering the Russian listening post.

"You are sure?" Crystal's gaze started by focusing on the bridge of Blade's nose. She wasn't entirely sober either. Then the gaze wandered downward, past Blade's chin, over his chest and stomach, and down a little farther. There it stopped.

Blade poured himself some more beer from the jug and raised the cup in salute. "I'm *very* sure."

As Blade drank, some of the beer slopped over the rim of the cup and fell onto his bare chest. Eye of Crystal knelt beside him, bent over his chest, and began licking the beer off Blade's skin. Her tongue darted in and out, lapping up the beer and wetting her full lips. They were very red lips, although the Uchendi used no cosmetics except the warriors' war paint.

That flickering tongue and its warm caresses on his skin were slowly hypnotizing Blade with pleasure. He hardly cared. Then the sensations of Crystal's tongue gave way to another one, stronger and more familiar. She was bending so low that her full breasts were pressing against his chest.

Blade felt small but firmly erect nipples and the lovely give of breasts changing shape under pressure. Crystal was also feeling it. Her eyes were closed, and one hand was now creeping down Blade's stomach.

Crystal unhooked Blade's loinguard and pushed it aside. She held Blade's manhood, warm fingers teasing as skillfully as the tongue. Blade groaned happily

"Strong enough, yes," she murmured.

Blade would have been almost past saying anything, but fortunately no words were needed. Eye of Crystal pulled away from Blade just long enough to untie the drawstring of her leather skirt, her only garment. It slid down over her well-rounded hips. As it reached the floor she stepped aside, too eager to move gracefully. She nearly fell, and

Blade had to reach up and balance her as she lowered herself into place.

Blade savored the moment of entry. He always had, from the first time he'd ever had a woman. There were lots of other pleasures in sex, of course, but this was certainly one of the biggest and best. From the way Crystal closed her eyes and let her mouth sag open, Blade suspected she felt the same.

In fact, this was the best Blade had ever felt. He couldn't put his finger on exactly why. So he put all his fingers on Crystal's breasts. They were skilled fingers, as quite a few women had told him. So did Crystal, although she didn't use words. She kept her eyes closed and moaned quietly, then not so quietly.

Blade tried to keep quiet for a while. He was just about to lose the fight when he realized what was happening to make this sex different from all the other times.

He and Crystal were in telepathic contact. Only slightly, less than he'd ever had with Cheeky, but now that he knew what to look for, he recognized the odd feeling in his mind. Odder than usual, because he had the sense of both entering and *being* entered, of being both himself and Crystal.

He gasped, partly in triumph, partly because he couldn't stay quiet any more. Then he realized something else. Crystal was close to her climax. Either she hadn't had a man in a long time or the telepathic link was increasing her pleasure.

It wasn't doing so badly for Blade, either. He knew that his own control was slipping—slipping, the devil! It was just about gone, he was on the edge, he was going over—

He stopped. Or rather, he was stopped. Crystal was not only in his mind, but she was passing through his mind into his body. Into one particular part of his body.

She was holding back his climax until she reached her own.

It made sense. Blade knew that, with the small part of

his mind that still held the power of reason. A very small part, by now. When it came to analytical thought, being on the verge of climax was almost as distracting as being in the middle of it.

He also wasn't sure he liked the sensation. Physically, it was marvelous. It was agony, but it was also delicious, and he wouldn't have minded it's going on for hours.

But this amount of control by the woman? For all Blade knew, the women were supposed to crack the whip in sex among the Uchendi. He had just enough old-fashioned male vanity to resent her control. He also had the sense to suppress his resentment because Crystal was reading his thoughts. She would detect any hostility.

Then she might retaliate. Blade doubted that his manhood was the only part of his body she could control while they were linked telepathically. Her father could certainly do more, and only sheer luck had saved Blade from harming the Guardian in their meeting. He wouldn't have the kind of control he needed to do that again, not this time, not with Crystal all around him, warm and tight and sliding furiously up and down, her pubic hair tickling him, swaying forward until her breasts brushed his chest, farther forward until she could bite his shoulder, her arms tightening around him until she was plastered against him. His control was going but so was hers. . . .

Blade didn't groan. He howled like a madman as his hips bucked and thrashed and pounded himself into Crystal. The woman clung frantically to him as her pelvis took on a life of its own, as if he was a log she had to ride through foaming rapids.

At last she screamed, a scream muffled in Blade's chest and her own hair. She screamed again, then the scream turned into happy sobbing.

At last Crystal was silent and Blade caught his breath. She lay on top of him, still snugly fitted to him, and giggled.

"I caught you by surprise, with the Voice. Didn't I, Blade?"

"You did."

"You say the Voice is not unknown among the English, just not lawful or much taught?"

"Yes. All the English women I knew who had the Voice were unlawful for me to bed. So I never had the Voice with a woman at the same time I was in her." He grinned. "Next time I'll know what I'm doing."

She laughed out loud. "You mean, this was your first time with a woman. You—ouch!" He pinched her admirably firm and rounded buttocks.

"No, it was not my first time bedding a woman. Nor will it be my last time bedding you."

"I certainly hope not!"

It wasn't.

Blade and Eye of Crystal took to each other with enthusiasm, tenderness, and laughter. Blade would have enjoyed her company even without the sex, or the sex without the telepathy. Having everything made it just that much better.

Crystal taught Blade a few things about telepathy in sex. He discovered that he could arouse her by simply projecting the image of her writhing in climax. She promptly returned the favor. They found that if she brought him to climax by fellatio while they were in contact, she would also climax, nine times out of ten.

They discovered a lot of other things, which Blade knew he would have to report to Lord Leighton when he got back home. They would make interesting reading, and not entirely because of their value for the study of telepathy. For the first time Blade didn't like the idea of talking about his sex life in Dimension X as frankly as the Project required. He'd be revealing things he'd never thought were there to be revealed!

However, that didn't alter the fact that he was learning

a lot about telepathy while he was having fun! If having Crystal's every little response written down in Lord Leighton's files helped give the Project controlled telepathy—well, they'd just have to be written down. This was all the more important, now that Cheeky was almost certainly gone for good.

Once he and Crystal became lovers, Blade found that he didn't think about Cheeky for days at a time, and when he did he didn't miss him as much as before. He wondered how much Crystal knew about Cheeky, and whether she was doing anything to affect his memory. Whether or not it was deliberate, he was grateful for the healing she was giving him.

Because he was so grateful, and for other reasons as well, Blade could never quite bring himself to explain to Crystal how soon he might have to leave her. She seemed to sense it anyway, and was remarkably cheerful about the prospect.

"We are good as we are, Blade. If we tried to be different, we might not be as good. My father says you are a man who has traveled far, and my Voice tells me the same. You would not wish to stop traveling, and if I asked you to you would be angry. Nor would I care to have as husband a man who might spend so much time away from my bed—Blade, have I hurt you?"

"No." How to explain about Zoé, who'd left him for just about that reason, with the Official Secrets Act buggering up things even worse? He'd thought that memory and its pain were dead and buried, until the Guardian's probe of his memories showed him otherwise.

Eye of Crystal wasn't worried about being loved and left, but her father worried for her. Or at least Kyarta told Blade that, as nearly as he could understand. The Guardian's wife was handsome and charming and by no means stupid. But she kept changing the subject on a whim, and she never used two words when five would do half as well.

"He thinks you ought to be named Distant Eagle,"

Kyarta said. "But that would be using an old name too soon after the man who brought it honor died." She spent the next ten minutes telling him about the dead warrior Distant Eagle, before remembering that his name had really been Gray Eagle.

"He fears I will travel on and leave Crystal grieving?" Blade finally asked.

"Oh, yes," she said. Another twenty minutes went by as Kyarta related tales of all the young women among the Uchendi who'd been loved and left during the last ten years, talking as if she'd known each one personally.

Blade felt his blood pressure rising, but kept his temper. He didn't want to annoy the woman. Like her husband, she would be a dangerous enemy, and she was telling him a lot of things about the Uchendi that just might be useful. He also suspected that she was a much better listener than she seemed, and would remember any slips of his tongue.

Finally, Kyarta ran down enough to say, "But I do not worry about Eye of Crystal. She knows what she's doing with you. She is strong." And that was that.

Of course Eye of Crystal was strong, Blade realized. After all, she'd reached the age of twenty living with this woman without going out of her mind. He wondered sometimes how the Guardian put up with her.

The Guardian would not bother Blade or his daughter as long as his wife insisted they be left alone. And River Over Stones was not going to go against the blessing the Guardian had given Blade. At least not in public, and so far he'd found no chance to do anything in private.

The rest of the warriors of the Uchendi seemed to be waiting to make up their minds about Blade. Or perhaps they were waiting for someone to help them decide? Blade suspected it was the latter. The warriors of the Uchendi were an independent-minded lot, but in some matters they followed their leaders.

Who was the key leader in this case? It didn't take Blade long to know it was Winter Owl.

The Guardian's brother-in-law was the most famous living warrior of the Uchendi, one of the dozen greatest the tribe had ever known. He hadn't said anything against Blade, but he hadn't said anything much for him either. As long as he held his tongue, the warriors would keep an open mind on the subject of Blade of the English.

All very well, as far as it went. An open mind meant safety for Blade, but it didn't help the Uchendi. The Rutari might declare war any day; certainly they would make more raids. Blade knew he could help, if they let him, by giving the Uchendi weapons and teaching them to use them to overcome the *shpugas*. Without those hairy menaces, the Rutari would be no match for the plainsmen.

He'd need Winter Owl's support for any such new weapons, though. Without it, none of the warriors would listen to him. Even worse, Winter Owl might see Blade as a menace to his authority and influence. Then he would speak out against Blade, even in the face of the Guardian's blessing. Blade might have to leave the Uchendi for his own safety, and they would have to face their enemies with their two leaders quarreling.

An ugly picture, it seemed to Blade. And easily avoided, if he could just win over Winter Owl.

But how?

Chapter 17

It sounded like a small war going on beyond the hill. *Ezintis*
bawled, men shouted, hooves thudded on hard-packed
ground, and every so often something went *thump* or
whuck. It couldn't be a Rutari raid, not this close to the
main village, but Blade was curious. He ran out of his hut,
hurried up the hill, and looked down on the field along the
bank of the stream beyond it.

More than two dozen Uchendi warriors were riding back
and forth on *ezintis*. Each warrior was guiding his *ezinti*
with one hand, and the other hand held something like a
polo mallet with a wicker cup on the end. They seemed to
be chasing small feathered balls around the field, trying to
catch them in the cups of their mallets. If they couldn't
do that, they'd whack each other or the *ezintis* with the
mallets. Blade saw two men go sprawling on the ground,
but both promptly got up again, cursing much too loudly
for injured men.

Blade was almost at the edge of the field before anyone
noticed him. Then someone shouted, scooped a ball into
his cup, and slammed the ball straight at Blade. Blade
didn't even have time to consider ducking. He felt a *whfffff*
as the ball nearly parted his hair.

"Hey, you—!" Blade shouted. He went on to describe
what the man's mother had eaten the night she conceived
him, who his father had been, and why no woman would

touch him. By the time Blade ran out of breath the man was laughing so hard he could barely stay on his mount. He rode over as Blade bent to pick up the ball.

"I am sorry, Blade. It seemed a good jest."

"Well, it was not you whose skull might have cracked," said Blade. The ball was solid brass, wrapped in leather and with feathers woven into the leather. The weight made it fly far, but the feathers made it fly wildly.

He tossed the ball back to the rider. "I have not seen this game played here before. What is it called?"

By now other riders had seen Blade and come up. "It is called *nor*," said one. "We are the White Tree team, or will be. We practiced to play against the Black Rock team of Winter Owl. Why do you ask, Blade? Is there a game like this in England?"

"There is, and I have played it." He hadn't played much polo, and none since he left Oxford. He didn't have the time or money to keep in practice, let alone maintain a stable of ponies.

Several riders exchanged significant looks. "Would you like to play for us?" said the same man.

"As a rider or as an *ezinti*?" said someone else, and there was laughter. "No, in truth," said the man, "you may laugh, but look at him. He could carry you on his shoulders for half a game, Friend of Lions! What *ezinti* could carry Blade? Certainly not mine, and I would not let him try, either. He may be needed for other work than carrying vast English warriors before long."

Everybody stopped smiling at the reminder that war with the Rutari could not be far off. Blade had to admit the man had a point. He weighed two hundred and ten pounds; most Uchendi warriors weighed a good deal less. He would be enough of a load for an *ezinti* to slow it down, and success in *nor* depended heavily on speed.

It wouldn't help, either, if he wound up playing against Winter Owl. He didn't know how important having his team win was to the warrior, but why take chances?

But why not take a chance? He couldn't go on sitting on his arse much longer, not with the Uchendi needing help. Even if he annoyed Winter Owl, there must be other warriors with some influence. Friend of Lions, captain of the White Tree team, might be one of them.

"I will play as one of the White Trees, if there is an *ezinti* fit to carry me. I will not need one who can carry me fast, as long as he can carry me for a full game."

"How can you hope to play at all, if you are slow?" said Friend of Lions. He sounded honestly confused. "That is not the way of *nor*."

"It is not the old way of *nor*, this I know," said Blade. "But the old way of a thing is not always the only way or even the best way." He was bluffing about the game of *nor*. He didn't have much idea of what he was going to do once he got on the back of an *ezinti*. He did want to start getting the Uchendi used to the idea of change, and this was too good an opening to miss.

Friend of Lions shrugged. "You are the best judge of what you can do, Blade. Perhaps you are not so good a judge of the game of *nor*, but I will give you my own second mount for your riding until the game." He grinned. "But if you kill it or hurt it past use, you shall go among the Rutari to find me a new mount."

That was the standard penalty for killing or stealing another man's *ezinti* among the Uchendi. To most men, it was as good as a death sentence. To Blade, it sounded almost like an opportunity to spy on the Rutari with the blessing of Uchendi custom.

That might be handy.

Don't get ahead of yourself, he told himself. *If you don't make a good showing in the game of* nor, *Friend will just take away your mount and you'll have even less honor than before.*

"Among the Uchendi, I shall be as one of them, unless the spirits of my English ancestors turn their faces away from me. Now, let me see this stick you use in the game of *nor*."

Blade quickly discovered that to him the cup-ended stick was much more important in the game of *nor* than good riding or a fast *ezinti*. Blade had a longer and stronger arm and a sharper eye than any of the Uchendi riders. He could pick up a ball faster than any and hurl it farther and more accurately at the goal. The goals were foot-wide holes set in the top of mounds of earth at either end of the field. The ball had to be thrown accurately into the hole, not just slammed toward it and allowed to roll in.

It was also to Blade's advantage that when he swung his stick against another rider, it hurt. In practice, he and everybody else pulled their blows. On the day of the game, everybody would be striking full force. Broken bones were common in the game of *nor*, and dead *ezintis* not infrequent. There had even been dead men, although Uchendi warriors were hard to kill.

"*Nor* seems to be how you people practice for war," said Blade one evening, after a practice session that left him with bruises all over and a split lip. He'd scored six goals, so he was feeling rather good in spite of the aches and pains.

"It is," agreed Friend of Lions. "But I do not know if the Guardian will allow us to use man-strikes with the sticks in this Great Game. The Rutari watch and wait, and all of our warriors must be whole and ready to fight when they come."

"That is so," said Blade. "But why doesn't the Guardian just give the order not to strike?"

"It might anger Winter Owl," said Friend of Lions. "His team has five of the strongest man-strikers of the Uchendi. They would lose much strength if they could not play as they usually do."

No need to ask if the Guardian feared to anger Winter Owl. Blade began to wish he hadn't sworn to play against the warrior's team. However, it was too late to back out now without letting down the White Trees. That would be just as bad as angering Winter Owl by helping to beat his team.

There was one consolation. Blade now had an *ezinti* of his own, a sturdy if rather slow-witted beast. He could ride out of the village any time he wanted privacy, as long as he was back before nightfall. He didn't need to ride very far before he had enough privacy to start testing with bow and arrows while he waited for the Great Game of *nor* to take place.

The bow was no problem. His harness made a good one, just as he'd expected. If it got too hard he would dip it in a cold stream to make it more flexible; if it got too soft he would lay it on a sun-heated rock. *Ezinti* sinew made a good bowstring, and he'd found reeds tough enough for arrows to use for demonstration and practice.

He'd want wooden arrows with stone or even bronze heads before the war started. Unless he could find a poison for them, pointed-reed arrows wouldn't do much damage to the *shpugas*. Those hairy hides would repel a light bullet, let alone most arrows! Newly trained archers couldn't hope to hit vital spots and cause any significant damage.

Feathers for the arrows were a problem. The Uchendi had several different kinds of domestic fowl, and Blade tried them all. He collected so many different feathers that the Guardian himself wondered why.

"Before the war with the Rutari comes, I must make a war bonnet of feathers in the English style," Blade said. "I must test each kind of feather with my magic, where it will not disturb the village. The Rutari would not let me do that. This is one reason why I left them."

"None of the Uchendi will speak against the ways of the English without answering to me," said the Guardian.

"I thank you," said Blade. He would have been even more grateful if the Guardian had promised to make the warriors speak *for* English ways. But the Guardian ruled the Uchendi only in matters of telepathy and religion, not war.

Eventually Blade discovered that the best feathers came from something called a greenfoot, about the size of a chicken and the shape of a goose, with a nasty temper but a delicious flavor when roasted. Blade fletched two dozen reed arrows with greenfoot feathers and made all the rest into the promised war bonnet. Then he took everything out to his chosen archery range in a little fold of hills south of the village.

He was a good archer, but he wanted to be even better before he demonstrated archery to the Uchendi. He had to show them not only that it existed, but that it would *work*.

Four days before the Great Game of *nor*, Blade reached his archery range. It was midmorning and he'd left the village before dawn, with his stomach empty except for a drink of water. The first thing he did was eat a handful of nuts and a slab of dried meat. Then he settled down to practice.

By noon he'd used all his arrows several times, broken four of them, and brought down two birds on the wing. He was particularly proud of that. The birds were no larger than quail, and he'd picked them off at fifty yards. The reed arrows were better than he'd expected, and if he could find a poison for them they might do a job even against the *shpugas*.

He decided to make up for missing breakfast by roasting the birds for lunch. He was squatting in the shadow of a boulder, plucking the birds, when he heard the faint scraping of feet on stone above him.

Blade jumped up and away from the boulder in a single motion, then snatched up his spear and drew his knife in a second one. Soft laughter answered him, and Eye of Crystal's head appeared over the top of the boulder. She was grinning complacently.

"How did you get here?"

"I followed your trail. A child could have done that."

"A child can follow anyone who does not think he is being followed." It was true that Blade hadn't bothered to hide his tracks. He hadn't thought he would need to, either. "Very well. I have not been wise. That does not tell me why you are here."

"I wanted to see what you were doing, so that I might tell my father if it was dangerous to the Uchendi."

"You took a big chance. Suppose it was so dangerous that I decided to kill you to keep you from talking about it?"

"I did not let you hear me until I knew it was not dangerous. I knew you would not kill me unless you thought I would put *you* in danger."

Blade couldn't deny that. In fact, he wasn't sure he'd rather not leave the Uchendi than speak a word against Eye of Crystal. He wasn't exactly in love with her, but he'd bend over backward not to hurt her.

"So what do you think of what I am doing, now that you have decided it is no danger to the Uchendi?"

"I think it might be a danger to the *shpugas* of the Rutari. Is that what you want it to be?" she asked with a sly smile.

Blade's well-trained sixth sense for other people's tricks told him there was something more behind Eye of Crystal's grin. Probably not dangerous, but something he needed to know. "Yes. You see clearly. But it is not ready to be taken to war against the *shpugas*, or anything more dangerous than those birds you saw me kill."

"I know. It cannot be taken to war at all, unless my mother's brother, Winter Owl, allows it. He has the last word in such matters of war."

Here it comes, thought Blade. "Why do you tell me what I already know? Do you think I have lost my wits?"

"No." She laughed. "At least I do not think that playing against Winter Owl's team in the Great Game of *nor* is a sign of madness. But if he also learns that you are making weapons-magic without telling him—Blade, what did you say?''

What Blade had muttered under his breath was, ''There must be something in the water of this Dimension!'' First Cheeky, now Eye of Crystal, playing at blackmail. ''I do not wish him to know this, indeed. Do you wish to tell him?''

''That depends.''

''On what?''

''On whether or not you take me with you when you go against the Rutari.''

''Into the war? You little—'' He counted to ten, then said, ''You are not a warrior. You would need much protection. Also, either River Over Stones or—''

Eye of Crystal spat and nearly hit Blade. She giggled at the expression on his face. ''I am sorry, Blade. But that is what I think of River Over Stones. He will not lift a finger, let alone a spear, to take me one step outside the village. And Winter Owl—he will have too much else to do, leading the warriors.''

''But—what makes you think I will not have just as much to do?''

''When Winter Owl speaks for all warriors to learn the new weapons-magic, you will teach them. When the warriors march, your work will be done. I will not take one moment of the days while you teach. The nights, perhaps, but not the days.

''When we march, though, you will be as one warrior among many. It will not be hard for you to let me see the battle. Not as hard as it will be to have Winter Owl speak for your new weapon, if I talk to him now.''

Blade gritted his teeth. How to convince this girl that she was putting her people in danger, just because she wanted to see a battle? If she told Winter Owl about his ''weapons-magic'' maybe Winter Owl would see reason, but he was even more likely to see Blade's superior knowledge of warfare as a flat-out challenge to his authority. That authority was something he valued; he'd won it by years of fighting and hunting and the pain of a dozen wounds. He would not take lightly any challenge to it by an English wizard-warrior.

Eye of Crystal sat down on top of the boulder, cross-legged, with her hands in her lap. She wore only her loinguard and in that position looked stark naked. There was a fine sheen of perspiration on the upper slopes of her breasts. . . .

Blade tore his eyes away from her and shrugged. "I will not defy your father, mother, or mother's brother if they do not allow me to take you into the battle. If I did that, I would probably die. Is that not so?" She nodded reluctantly. "Then I would not be able to protect you. Otherwise, I swear to do my best to see that you march with me against the Rutari. Is that enough?" He did not add the thought, *It had bloody well better be!*

"Oh, yes," said Crystal. "I know you are only a man, as good a one as you are. I will not ask for more than a man can give."

"At least you haven't since the night before last," said Blade with a grin.

"Have you missed it?" she said with a laugh. Then before he could answer she leaped down from the top of the boulder, as lightly as a gazelle. In landing she managed to fall against him and throw her arms around him, while nuzzling his throat with her lips and pressing her breasts against his chest.

He lifted her and carried her off in search of soft ground. They didn't go fast, because he was kissing her breasts, and she had her hand under Blade's loinguard as they moved. By the time they got to a grassy stretch of the bank of the stream it didn't really matter whether they were in telepathic contact or not. They were both so eager that they pulled each other down and were locked together in moments, laughing and giggling, then sighing, groaning, and finally crying out in release. Crystal's happy scream was so loud that birds flew up in panic from around the bend of the stream.

They lay with Crystal draped across Blade's chest like a warm blanket. He ran a finger down her spine and played with her buttocks and the crease between them. "So tell me, Woman Who Asks More Than A Man Can Give, what news from the village? I've spent all my waking time either practicing archery or *nor*."

"There is a *hiba-gan* coming, or so we hear from the north." Something in Crystal's voice made Blade leave off caressing her.

"A what?"

"More likely a who. A *hiba-gan*, a Holy Wanderer. It does not come often. It is to be hoped it will pass through our village. Yet it is unlawful to send to it and ask."

"That doesn't tell me much," said Blade cautiously.

"There is not much to tell about this *hiba-gan* or any other," said Crystal. "They go where they will, sometimes bringing messages, sometimes only watching in silence. It is said that the message of the gods, which sends them wandering, changes their faces and skins, so they must cloak themselves from human eyes."

"They go about in disguise?"

"Oh yes. One cannot tell whether they are man or woman, or even human or beast, although they walk upright like men." She sat up. "Blade, are you thinking of uncloaking a Holy Wanderer?"

"I was not. I was thinking that this is perhaps not a good time for someone we are not sure about to learn the secrets of the Uchendi. Such as this." He slapped the bow.

"*Hiba-gans* do not heed matters of war," said Crystal. "And it is almost as unlawful to lie to one as it is to uncloak it. You would be cast out from the Uchendi if you did either, and your archery would be declared forbidden—"

Blade held up a hand. "Wait, wait, Crystal. I am not going to lie to the *hiba-gan*, nor uncloak it. Have I shown so little respect for the laws of the Uchendi or been so stupid that you would think that?" Seeing her shake her head slowly, he went on. "Nor do I ask anyone else to do these unlawful things. I merely ask that you not mention my archery to the *hiba-gan*, any more than you would to Winter Owl."

"And if the Holy Wanderer asks—then perhaps the *hiba-gan* is not what it seems, is perhaps trying to learn our secrets. . . ."

Very sharp, thought Blade. *Good thing she's on my side.* "Yes. Who knows? The *hiba-gans* might really be Idol Makers in disguise, come back to watch how the tribes are living. We do not know what the Idol Makers would think of me or my archery."

Crystal looked unsure if she should laugh or not. Finally she compromised with a thin smile. "That could be so," she said.

Blade gave up hope of the Uchendi being more willing than the Rutari to talk about the Idol, and decided he really shouldn't be surprised. It was probably a touchy subject for them.

Also, for all he knew, the Idol Makers might have been just a band of explorers passing through, with a technology that was advanced enough to look like magic to these tribesmen.

But I bloody well am going to find out for sure, before I leave this Dimension!

Chapter 18

The first of three periods of the Great Game of *nor* between the White Trees and the Black Rocks was nearly over. The score was five to three in favor of the White Trees, which meant Winter Owl was losing.

Blade scored three of his team's five goals. He'd scored two by simply hitting the hole from a distance so much greater than usual that none of the Black Rocks were watching him. They only realized he'd scored when the ball sailed into the hole, and all the people with bets on the White Trees cheered.

The people with bets on the Black Rocks groaned, and some of them shook their fists at Blade. Winter Owl himself didn't make a sound or a gesture—he would be the stoic Uchendi warrior to the end, even if an enemy was cutting him open with a dull knife. Sometimes, though, Blade saw him grimace when he didn't think anyone was looking at him.

Friend of Lions had predicted correctly; the Guardian had forbidden the *nor* players to use their sticks on each other. He hadn't forbidden punches, kicks, or trying to ride the other side down. The two masses of riders repeatedly crashed together, turning the game into something like a barroom brawl.

The White Trees advanced down the field again, with Friend of Lions shrieking war cries as if he were attacking a deadly enemy. He waved his stick like a cavalry sword, then lowered it as the two masses of riders pounded toward each other. Blade stayed out of this scrimmage. He was riding a large, strong *ezinti*, but it still had a job carrying him fast enough to keep him in the game at all. He wasn't sure if he wanted the Black Rocks to lose this game. He was damned sure he didn't want them to lose it through anything they could blame on him. That would give him a whole team of enemies, not to mention all the people who'd lose their bets.

The period came to an end before the teams got untangled. Blade could have easily scored another goal—the Black Rocks seemed to have forgotten completely that they *had* a hole to defend. However, he'd been in reach of the ball only a couple of times. It wouldn't be hard to convince his teammates he hadn't even seen it.

As he rode back to the White Trees end of the field, Blade scanned the crowd for the *hiba-gan*. There he—she—*it* was, right where it had been when the game started. It was still swathed in a rawhide cloak and hood that covered it from head to foot. When it did move, it moved slowly but steadily; there was nothing in its movements to prove it wasn't human. For now Blade was inclined to give the Holy Wanderer the benefit of the doubt in this matter.

River Over Stones was also stationed in the same place he'd been when the game started—ten feet to the right of the *hiba-gan*. His hands were crossed reverently on his stomach, and his eyes never left the shrouded figure. Since the *hiba-gan* came to the village two days ago, River had appointed himself its escort and protector. Since yesterday, it seemed that the *hiba-gan* had accepted this.

Being such an escort to a Holy Wanderer was a great honor and a sacred task. Many said that it was a sign the Spirits had forgiven River Over Stones for his opposition to Blade. So far no one was saying that it proved he might have been right about Blade after all.

On the other hand, no one said River Over Stones might be forcing himself on the *hiba-gan* to try and win back some of the honor he'd lost through opposing Blade. *Hiba-gans* were too much revered, and it was said their Voices were so powerful that deception was impossible. As for anyone even hinting that the *hiba-gan* might not be what it seemed, and that River Over Stones might be plotting with it—well, Blade didn't expect anyone to want to be burned at the stake for heresy. He didn't much care for the idea himself.

One thing about the *hiba-gan* had changed since the beginning of the game. It had put down the large leather sack it carried on a strap across its back. The sack now lay beside it on the gravel. Blade wasn't sure if it was just his imagination, or if the sack really did bulge oddly, as if there were something strangely shaped inside it.

Blade took several deep breaths and made his mind as blank as he could. He didn't use all his mental control; that would surely be detected by someone in the crowd and word sent to the Guardian. Blade wasn't sure what he was allowed to do by way of using the Voice, and he certainly didn't want to attract attention now.

With a blank mind he looked quickly back at the sack. No doubt about it. The bulge was in a different part of the sack—as if what was inside the bag had moved.

The sun was hot, but for a moment Blade felt cold. His mental control very nearly deserted him. Whatever was in the sack was alive. He'd never heard of a *hiba-gan* carrying a live animal in a sack with it. Why was the *hiba-gan* doing something unknown on its visit to the Uchendi, just after Blade came to them and right before the war with the Rutari . . . ?

It didn't add up. Or rather, it added up to something that had to be investigated. Openly if possible, secretly if not. Openly would be safer for Blade. That meant getting Winter Owl on his side. Doing anything against the *hiba-gan* would mean bending the law. If Winter Owl opposed that, nothing could be done—at least not to the *hiba-gan.*

Winning over Winter Owl meant one thing: The White Trees were going to have to lose this game of *nor*.

The two teams rode back onto the field for the second period. Blade stayed back toward the White Trees' rear, as if his *ezinti* were tiring. If he was careful, that would be the truth before anyone could get suspicious. Once the scrimmage began, most riders were too busy looking for the ball and for opposing players to worry about Blade.

Winter Owl must have given the Black Rocks a pep talk. They charged down on their opponents so hard that a few riders pulled up to save their mounts. This gave Winter Owl a clear shot at the White Trees' goal. He took it. The ball whipped past Blade like a bullet and *plunked* into the hole.

One of the White Trees rode up to Blade, grumbling, "You were the closest, Blade. Couldn't you have stopped that one?"

"Nonsense," said Friend of Lions. "The ball was in the hole before Blade could have been in its path."

"Yes," said Blade. "If I had arms fifteen feet long I might have stopped it." He shrugged. "Nobody ever said the Black Rocks were going to be easy. Or at least I never did."

They rode back into the scrimmage. This time the two teams were evenly matched, until suddenly the tangle spewed out a Black Rock with the ball in his cup. Blade recognized him. He was one of the younger players and so far hadn't done a thing to make himself look dangerous.

Now, though, he had a clear path to the goal. Blade dug his heels into his *ezinti*. He was the best-placed White Tree to stop the young ballcarrier. If he didn't move, someone might become suspicious.

Luck was with Blade. His *ezinti* now really was tiring under his weight. He didn't have to rein it in more than twice. He was still a good ten feet behind the young rider when the other man flipped the ball toward the White Trees' hole. At that distance a drunken one-eyed man could have made the goal.

Blade rode back, listening to the cheers of the Black Rocks' supporters and the groans of the people with money on the White Trees. He didn't hear anyone mention his name. After all, he'd been the only one of the White Trees who even *tried* to stop the goal. The fact that his *ezinti* wasn't fast enough was hardly his fault.

Fault or no fault, however, the game was now tied at five to five. Winter Owl was no longer being the stoic warrior. He was grinning so widely that Blade began thinking maybe he had a chance of getting him on his side.

Now it was the White Trees' turn to get a brief pep talk from their captain. Friend of Lions made such a rousing speech that it had everyone cheering, including Blade. He wasn't entirely faking, either. Damn it, these people deserved to win! They'd put blood, sweat, and tears into both training and playing.

And if he was wrong about the *hiba-gan* . . . Blade was pretty sure he wasn't, though. And if he was right about the Holy Wanderer being up to tricks—well, there were more important things at stake for the Uchendi than who won today's game. Blade was gritting his teeth as he rode back into the game.

The pep talk worked so well that the White Trees promptly scored a goal without Blade's getting within twenty feet of the ball. Then Friend of Lions scored a second, and the Black Rocks came back and scored one of their own, both teams crippling several *ezintis*, which left them short-handed. . . .

That made the score seven to six in favor of the White Trees. The crowd was silent now. Half were too hoarse and breathless to cheer, the other half too excited, too aware they were seeing an extraordinary game.

Blade would have been happier if they'd gone on cheering. In this silence, there could be a thousand eyes ready to fix themselves on the man who had the ball, watching for something to praise or criticize. Throwing the game under these conditions was going to be trickier than he'd expected.

The scrimmage that left both teams short-handed also made them cautious for the rest of the second period. There were no more goals or casualties on either side. Although he never had the ball, Blade rode around vigorously, to make sure his *ezinti* stayed tired.

The last period of the game was only minutes old when Blade suddenly found himself with the ball in the cup of his stick. Some weird twist of fate or puff of wind had landed it there. Blade couldn't just dump it out, so he got rid of it the only way he could—with a shot at the goal. It was a long shot even for Blade, and it would have been simply foolish for anyone else to try.

So nobody was surprised when the ball bounced off the base of the cone and rolled back onto the field. One of the Black Rocks picked it up and pounded down the field behind his teammates as if the Devil was at the heels of his mount.

Blade had to stay in the scrimmage. If he pulled out and the man scored with the ball he himself had virtually given to the other team, he was going to be noticed. So Blade stayed in close and even used knees and elbows against some of the Black Rocks. He'd worked out how to use unarmed-combat techniques from horseback, although not how to pull his punches. At least none of the Uchendi would recognize Home Dimension martial arts!

Blade dismounted one man and disabled another's mount. Then the Black Rock rider took his shot at the goal and missed. Blade joined the cheering, then saw the Guardian signaling from the sidelines. A break was called, while Blade rode over and submitted to a tongue-lashing from the shaman.

"Have you less honor or sense of shame than I thought,

Blade?'' the older man growled. ''Are you so eager to win that you will risk killing a warrior of the Uchendi?''

And much more in the same vein. Blade thought afterward that one of the hardest things he did that day was listen to the Guardian with a completely straight face. It was also one of the most important. The Guardian could read faces as well as minds to learn what other men were thinking.

Finally the Guardian ran out of things to say, dismissed Blade, and turned back to Kyarta and Eye of Crystal. As Blade urged his mount back on to the field, Crystal winked at him. That made him feel better.

Friend of Lions greeted him as he rejoined the team. ''That was bad luck, your long shot missing,'' he said. He sounded more disappointed than angry.

Blade shrugged. ''It was. But at least they did us no great harm with it. A long arm and a clear opening do not make me Superman, after all.''

''Who is Superman?''

''A legendary hero of the English. He has the strength of many men, he flies, and can see through walls.''

Friend of Lions seemed impressed. ''I wonder—could he have been one of the Idol Makers?''

''We have no legends of visitors by that name,'' said Blade cautiously. ''More than that I could not say.''

''More than that it might not be wise to say,'' said Friend. ''Here on the *nor* field the Spirits are always listening. If they wish to avenge an insult they do not find it hard.''

Then the whistles and drums began to sound, calling the teams back to their positions for the rest of the game. Both teams were now tired riders on tired mounts. No one could have detected this from the way the Black Rocks came on, though. Winter Owl was far ahead, taking all sorts of chances he would probably not have risked if sticks had been lawful weapons today.

''Curse these child's rules!'' growled Friend of Lions at

the sight. "If I could shove my stick a hand's breadth up his arse he'd not be sitting so easy!" He clearly wanted to say more, but that would have been too close to disputing the Guardian's judgment.

By now the day had turned blazing hot, and two dozen *ezintis* were churning up the field until a fog of dust hung over it. It was getting hard to see one's own teammates, and nearly impossible to find the ball unless it hit you between the eyes. *And if that happens, you won't be able to use your knowledge of the huba-gan,* thought Blade. Half a pound of bronze moving at the speed of a cricket ball would crack a man's skull like a hammer.

Everyone was riding cautiously. Exhausted mounts and poor visibility increased the danger of being spilled and trampled. Blade didn't have to worry about standing out in the crowd any more. Nobody more than thirty feet away would have recognized him, let alone told what he was doing. He was coated with dust from head to foot, to the roots of his hair and even under his loinguard. His mouth was filled with dust, and mud dripped from his limbs where sweat had flowed through the dust.

A Black Rock scored; the game was tied again. Blade hoped all of the White Trees were even more exhausted than he was. If they scored again, it was going to take a lot of luck for either him or the Black Rocks to save the game. He wasn't sure if the best thing for him now wouldn't be his mount dropping dead.

It was the first time in his life that Blade had thought playing the game out to the end would not be a good thing. Most of the time it was the wisest course of action. You always should be able to outlast an opponent, if nothing else. But not now. Not when Winter Owl's goodwill might mean the difference between victory and something far worse.

Winter Owl found himself in the open, with the ball and a long clear shot. He let fly, and the ball hit home.

Eight to seven, in favor of the Black Rocks. Some of the

Black Rocks supporters were cheering again. They had a right to, Blade realized. The game had about five minutes more to run, and if the Black Rocks simply played it cautiously they would have their victory. Then Richard Blade would have a good-tempered Winter Owl ready to listen to him.

Half blinded by dust, sweat, and heat, men on both sides were now riding their mounts over the boundaries of the field and being ruled out of the game. The Black Rocks were down to seven riders, the White Trees to six. Blade hoped the next rider would be from the White Trees. That would settle matters.

A Black Rock charged at him out of the murk. Blade raised his stick. The other mount flinched aside, nearly went down, then headed off at an angle. The rider cursed. Blade saw now the bedraggled feathers of the ball trailing from the cup of his stick. He dug his heels into his mount's flank and followed the Black Rock.

Better keep an eye on him, to make sure he doesn't do anything stupid like giving the White Trees a chance to score, Blade told himself. *Just don't get caught in a position where what you can do will make the difference between winning and losing.*

Suddenly the runaway *ezinti* was coming up on the boundary of the field. The rider had to get rid of the ball and did so, to the nearest rider—Blade. Perhaps he hadn't recognized Blade as a White Tree, or was too exhausted to think that a rider following him might not be a friend.

As he realized this ugly truth, a drum started to boom, loud enough to be heard all over the field. When that drum sounded thirty times, the game would be over. There was no tie in the game of *nor;* if the score was even at the end of three periods there would be a fourth. Blade wanted to avoid that. If he could just keep from scoring until those thirty beats passed . . .

He couldn't drop the ball. All at once there wasn't enough dust around him to hide him from his teammates.

They would see him plainly. His mount seemed to have found new strength. It was pawing at the ground, ready to run instead of collapse. Blade cursed it.

If only he had some really useful form of telepathy! Telekinesis, for example—the ability to control physical objects with the mind. He could shoot the ball and make it miss, or snap his stick before the ball left the cup, or—But he didn't have telekinesis, and someone would surely detect it if he did and used it. Using telepathy among telepaths was like shouting secrets in a crowded theater.

Blade urged his mount down the field. There wasn't anything to do except his best, and hope it wouldn't be good enough. Twenty beats to go, nineteen, eighteen, seventeen—the goal almost within shooting distance—fifteen, fourteen, thirteen, twelve—

If he shot now he might miss. But he didn't have to shoot now, and everybody would wonder if he did. He had a clear field ahead. He could ride down and practically spit the ball into the cup, and since it was possible he had to do it. Blade rode on.

At eight beats to go he was in shooting range. He dipped his stick, then snapped it upward. The ball soared through the air, losing a feather at it went. Maybe that would change its course enough to make it miss. It rose—and suddenly Blade knew that it was rising higher than it should. He hadn't put that much strength into the stick's movements, hoping the ball would fall short.

Instead the ball rose a good six feet into the air. Nobody except Blade would have noticed anything, but Blade stared as the ball soared over the hole. It struck on the far side of the mound, bounced so high that Blade was afraid for a moment it was going to do the impossible and bounce back in, then rolled down the mound and off into the coarse grass beyond the boundaries of the field.

The roar of the crowd drowned out the last few drumbeats.

The Black Rocks had won the Great Game of *nor*, eight to seven.

Blade threw down his stick in a good imitation of anger. He was more surprised and suspicious than angry. Something—or someone—had obviously been acting on the ball from outside. Telekinesis? Probably. And whose? Had he managed to become telekinetic by simply wanting to be? Or had someone else—?

For the moment it was an unanswerable question, even if he could give it the attention it deserved. Both teams were riding toward him, their captains riding side by side in the rear. Both sides looked too exhausted to either rejoice at their victory or mourn their defeat. All Blade saw was blank, dust-caked faces like his own.

All except Winter Owl's. The warrior was grinning as he rode up to Blade. "Blade, if you play for the White Trees next year, I think I shall call the game their victory before we play. Why make ourselves tired and dirty when we know what will happen? Better to sit with women on our knees and beer in our bellies."

"Do not be so sure of that," Friend of Lions said. He wasn't exactly grinning, but he no longer looked grim. "And besides, does not the beer taste better when one has worked up a proper thirst?"

"There may be something in that," said Winter Owl. "Let us go find out for certain, and take Blade with us. This day I say there is neither winner nor loser in the Great Game of *nor*."

"I thank you," said Blade. He had to fight not to sway on the back of his mount, and the idea of *anything* to drink was enticing.

His day's work was done. He had Winter Owl's goodwill, and no one suspected there was anything odd about the outcome of the game. No one, that is, except the person who jiggled the ball in Blade's last shot—if there was such a person.

That question could wait. Eye of Crystal was running

across the field toward him, wearing a broad grin and not much else. She laughed and threw her arms around his knee, and he reached down and tousled her hair. She would make a fine woman to have on his knee while he quenched his thirst.

Chapter 19

By the time the Mistress Ellspa was asleep, it was dark. If things were not the way they were, Cheeky would have been afraid to leave the hut in the darkness. But he had to go to the Uchendi village to find the Master Blade and tell him what he knew.

The Wise One had gone into the Uchendi village with Moyla, leaving Ellspa and Cheeky a short distance away, in case she needed them. The feather-monkey and his mistress were staying in a deserted hut in the woods not far from the village, awaiting word from the Wise One.

Cheeky had learned what was afoot from Moyla, who had sent a message to him. (Apparently telepathy worked over long distances, like radio transmission.) What Moyla had said was that tonight, the Mistress Wise One was going to send another Master—Cheeky had the picture of a young man who seemed to be angry all the time—to kill the Master Blade. If Cheeky did not go to the village and give a warning, the Master Blade might die. Cheeky could not let that happen, no matter how dangerous it might be to try to stop it.

Cautiously Cheeky crept out from under the blanket he shared with Ellspa and looked up at the roof, which was full of holes. He could see that the moon was in the sky. Maybe it would not be quite as dark as he had feared. But animals would be walking in the night bigger than he was and hungry enough to eat him. He could not see the mountains that during the day would have guided him to the village of the Uchendi Masters and the Master Blade. He might get lost. Then he would die even if he did not meet a dangerous animal.

The Mistress Ellspa sighed softly and stretched out her arms on either side. One hand nearly touched Cheeky's back. He stayed very still and took small breaths until he was sure the Mistress was still asleep.

Cheeky wondered if he should try to mind-speak the Mistress Ellspa without her knowledge. He might be able to do it. If he could, he might be able to make sure she slept so deeply that she would not wake up until long after he was in the village. That would be better for him, since then she could not warn the Wise One. It might also be better for Ellspa because the Wise One would not be so angry with her if she was put to sleep.

Cheeky did not want anyone angry with Ellspa. She had always been kind to him, not only in what she did but in what she thought. She really liked him, so much that he had sometimes heard her thinking that she wished he was a man. He had wished that she was one of the Feather People.

That could not be. Also, she was not kind to the Master Blade. She was still his enemy, and she would help to kill him if she could. He did not even try to talk to her about this. She would not change her mind, and she would tell the Wise One what he felt. The Mistress Wise One was not kind to anyone except Moyla, and not always kind to her. The Wise One would be sure to have Cheeky killed, or at least keep him from escaping.

He decided that he would not try to speak to Ellspa's mind. He knew more about strong thoughts, both his own and the Masters', than he did about mind-speaking. He was not sure he could enter a Master's mind without the Master knowing and stay there until the Master did something he or she did not want to do. So he would just go out of the hut now and hope that the moon would let him go to the village before Ellspa woke up.

Fortunately the hut was so ruined that there were many ways out. Cheeky used a gap between two logs. It was tight, but he finally got out with rumpled feathers and a few bruises. The ground outside the hole was hard, not soft like the ground outside the door to the hut. He would not leave any footprints on the hard ground. Beyond that was forest where he would also be hard to follow. He would not stay in the forest long, though—he did not want to lose his way.

Cheeky hurried across the ground toward the trees. At every step he expected to hear Ellspa shout, either in his mind or with her mouth. Instead there was silence all the way to the forest, and even after he got inside it.

Inside the trees it was very dark on the ground, but overhead he could sometimes see the moon through the branches. He scrambled up a tree until he was the height of six or seven Masters. Now he could see the moon even better, and there might not be any dangerous animals up here. Birds, yes—he remembered the hawks the Masters of the Crimson River sometimes used. But nothing else would be up this high unless it could climb trees as well as he could.

Cheeky started swinging through the forest, from branch to branch and from tree to tree. He was happy to be able to move like this, in the old way of the Feather People. He was not so happy that he forgot about the Master Blade, the danger to him, and the warning he must bring.

Blade awoke to the sense of something warm close to him. He wasn't surprised to find that it was Eye of Crystal snuggled against him, her bare rump pressed comfortably against his stomach. His hand crept over her shoulder and down to cup one full breast.

"*Yeeeeep?*" came a soft sound from the darkness around the sleeping furs.

Suddenly Blade wasn't sure that he was awake after all.

That sound was so much like Cheeky, but he was hundreds of miles away with the Rutari. There had to be some other explanation.

("No, Master. It is me, Cheeky. I have come back. I want to stay with you.")

In that moment Blade took back a good many of the things he'd said against telepathy. Cheeky's mental voice was absolutely unmistakable, and the darkness of the hut didn't make any difference. No problems with identification, as long as the other telepath wanted to be identified.

That started a train of thought that brought Blade wide awake and up out of the furs in a moment. Crystal murmured and rolled over, but didn't wake up. Blade hoped she would stay asleep until he'd finished talking with Cheeky.

("How did you get here? Did you escape from the Rutari?")

("I left the Mistress Ellspa. She is in an empty hut that is all broken, about half a night's walk for me from here. The Mistress Wise One and Moyla are here in the village. The Mistress Wise One wears Master-skins to make you think she is something she is not. She hides—")

Blade let out an oath that would have blistered the paint on the hut if there'd been any, and jumped to his feet. This woke Eye of Crystal. She sat up, naked and staring at Blade as if he'd gone crazy.

"I was right about the *hiba-gan*! It's no Holy Wanderer! It's the Wise One of the Rutari in disguise. She's got River Over Stones as an ally and they're planning to kill me!"

"Blade, what in the name of all Wisdom are you talking about?"

Blade took a deep breath. "I don't have time to explain more than once." He repeated Cheeky's message, while Crystal stared alternately at him and at Cheeky. She seemed uncertain that the feather-monkey was really there, and kept rubbing her eyes as if this might just possibly make him go away.

When Blade was finished and it was obvious Cheeky was real, Crystal put on her loinguard and tucked her knife into it. She didn't bother with sandals or headband.

"I think you are telling the truth, or at least what you believe to be the truth," she said. "However this may be, I must go with you. You do not know all the laws and customs, and you may need someone to speak of what we see."

In other words, a witness. Blade nodded. "That is true. But you do not need to come into danger with me. Your father—"

"It would take time to wake up my father and bring him. If what you say is the truth, we do not have the time. If you have been told a lie, then there will be no need for the Guardian." She stood on tiptoe to kiss him. "Besides, you swore you would take me to the war with you. Is this not the first battle of the war with the Rutari?"

Blade knew he wouldn't win this argument. "All right. Come on. But don't get too close to me. We may both have to move fast."

He turned to Cheeky. ("You come with me. Ride on my shoulder until we get to the Wise One's hut. Then get down and do not get in my way.")

("You do not think good of me again?")

("I do not think much of you at all until we have fought the Wise One. Is that not also wise?")

("Oh, yes.")

Crystal's eyes widened as Cheeky jumped onto Blade's shoulder, but she said nothing. Either she hadn't overheard the telepathic conversation, or she knew there was no time to waste satisfying her curiousity.

Blade would have liked to explain Cheeky to Crystal. He would have liked even more to have Cheeky explain how he'd been getting along among the Rutari. That might tell him something he hadn't known about the Wise

One. Again, the problem was no time. If Ellspa had noticed that Cheeky was gone and communicated with the Wise One, the older woman might already be alert and waiting.

If she is, Blade thought, *bugger the laws about dealing with* hiba-gans. *I'll knock her flat and sit on her until I finish explaining who she is. Somehow I don't think those laws were meant to protect spies and assassins disguised as Holy Wanderers.*

The *hiba-gan's* hut was at the far end of an isolated cluster of buildings on the riverbank, upstream from the walled village. This was traditional—Holy Wanderers were expected to keep themselves a little apart from the people they visited. This was good luck for Blade. He got there without having to explain Cheeky or his mission to the guards at the four gates of the village or people on the streets.

Twenty yards from the hut, Blade put Cheeky down. The feather-monkey fell back while Crystal came forward to stand on Blade's left. For a moment Blade again savored the unusual sensation of not having to go into battle alone. Then he charged straight at the door of the hut.

Blade's two hundred and ten fast-moving pounds hit the hut door like a battering ram. The door's hinges were leather thongs and they snapped like thread. The door not only flew off its hinges, it flew clear across the hut and smashed itself to kindling wood against the far wall.

There were two people in the middle of the hut, the Wise One and River Over Stones. The Wise One wore nothing but her scars and a head band, and was riding astride River, who wore about the same. Lost in lust for the moment, neither of them even looked up until the flying door hit the far wall.

Moyla wasn't so pleasantly busy and was more alert. Out of the corner of his eye Blade saw her snatch up something, then dart toward him. As she moved, he also heard a wordless screech in his mind.

("Master! Moyla dangerous!")

Blade couldn't see how a creature even smaller and weaker than Cheeky could possibly be dangerous, but he was too well trained to ignore any warning. He remembered what one of his combat instructors said: React first, evaluate afterward, and you just may live to die in bed.

Blade leaped high and to one side as Moyla came at him. She could turn practically on a dust mote, though, and changed course to match Blade's movements. He had time to see she was holding something in her hand, long and thin with a glistening black tip.

Then Cheeky darted between Blade's legs and ran against Moyla so hard that she bounced off him like a billiard ball. The black-tipped object flew out of her paw and landed on the floor. Cheeky jumped on top of it, arms outstretched to fend Moyla off without hurting her. His crest was laid back, though, and his mouth was open to show all his teeth.

Moyla ignored Cheeky's obvious distaste for a fight to the death. She came at him again and grappled, trying to get him away from her weapon. Cheeky refused to be budged. The feather-monkey and his ex-girlfriend rolled over and over, screeching and clawing at each other until fur and feathers flew.

By this time the two humans were also alert. The Wise One's techniques of mental control got her ready to fight faster. Blade saw her leap to her feet, a knife in her hand. She would be fast and probably dangerous with it, even more dangerous if she had time to use her telepathic weapons.

The blunders of her ally and lover kept her from using either. River Over Stones lurched to his feet, holding a spear and shouting obscene curses at Eye of Crystal. Any fool could have seen that he was in no shape to fight, and Eye of Crystal was the first to take action. She brushed past Blade, closed with River, and kicked him smartly between the legs.

River's scream froze everyone in the hut except Blade and Cheeky. Blade snatched up River's spear as the young man doubled up. He was tempted to return it at once to its owner, point first, but he remembered in time that River Over Stones owed his people an explanation and ought to be kept alive long enough to give it. So he reversed the spear and slammed the butt down on River's skull. The man crumpled and flopped to the floor almost at Blade's feet, twitching and writhing as the agony in his groin penetrated even his half-numb brain.

Meanwhile, Cheeky got on top of Moyla and pounded her head against the hard earth of the hut floor until she went limp. For a moment he knelt beside her, making little noises that might have meant anything. He wasn't sending any telepathic messages, and Blade certainly wasn't going to intrude on his mind at this time anyway. If he'd had any doubts about the sincerity of Cheeky's return and loyalty, they were now forever laid to rest.

After a moment he bent down, patted Cheeky gently on the head, and picked up Moyla's weapon. It was a long thin dagger, almost a needle, with its point covered for several inches with something black and glistening like tar. Blade didn't try to examine it closely or wipe it off; he merely wedged the dagger into a chink in the logs where it couldn't be stepped on or grabbed by an enemy.

Two of the three enemies were in no shape to grab anything. A sudden wail from Cheeky told Blade that Moyla was dead, while River Over Stones had passed out from pain. While Blade kept an eye on the Wise One, Eye of Crystal dragged River to the door, tore up her loinguard, and tied him hand and foot with the strips. Blade stopped worrying about the girl's handling herself in action.

While all this was happening, the Wise One was standing by the tangled furs and skins on the floor. Except for the rise and fall of her breasts and the sweat on her thighs, she might have been a statue. Blade was careful to avoid meeting her eyes. He wasn't sure what telepathic weapons she might have, but he wasn't going to give any of them a chance.

Then the footsteps of what sounded like half the village thudded outside, and the doorway was suddenly filled with people. Blade wasn't surprised, since River Over Stones had made enough noise to be heard for miles. Eye of Crystal was nearly knocked down, and Cheeky had to jump onto Blade's shoulder to keep from being trampled.

"This is no true *hiba-gan*," said Blade. "This is the Wise One of the Rutari. She came here disguised as a *hiba-gan* to kill me for fleeing from the unlawful ways of the Rutari. Not far from here her friend Ellspa waits to help her."

"She could still have taken a *hiba-gan's* vows," said someone outside.

"She has not," said Crystal. "When we entered, she and River Over Stones were as man and woman. *Hiba-gans* are celibate."

A long sigh issued from the crowd. Then Winter Owl's voice rose above it. "Make way for the Guardian!"

The warrior and the shaman marched into the hut side by side, and Blade stepped clear to give them room to face the Wise One. For the first time, the woman seemed uneasy. She'd been prepared for death or torture, but to see her one equal among all the telepaths of Latan facing her was another matter, particularly without Moyla. She licked her lips.

"I have heard everything," said the Guardian, "and your life is mine to take as I will. You know this is true. You came here to do murder, without an oath protecting you, and disguised as a Holy Wanderer. Three times over, your life is mine to take."

"That is so," said the Wise One. It was the first sound she made.

"But I will not give you to Winter Owl or to Blade of

England to kill slowly,'' the Guardian went on. ''Instead, I give Challenge. Meet my Challenge, here and now, without calling your friend Ellspa, and if you win, you may go free.''

The Wise One's eyes widened in surprise. ''You swear this by the Wisdom?''

''Father—!'' began Eye of Crystal, but Winter Owl gripped her arm.

''Do not shame him,'' he whispered, so low that he probably thought no one heard him, and indeed no one except Blade did.

''Better dead than shamed?'' Crystal replied in the same tone.

''Yes.''

She muttered something that sounded like a curse on all men in general, but then fell silent.

''I swear by the Wisdom that this shall be the Fourth Challenge,'' said the Guardian.

''Then I shall meet you as Wise Ones and Guardians have met thrice before, and Ellspa shall not know of this.'' She knelt and spread her hands on the ground. The Guardian knelt and spread his hands on top of hers. The Wise One was so graceful that Blade's mind flashed back to how he'd held that slim brown body locked to his.

After that there was nothing for everyone except the two shamans to do except leave the hut and let the Challenge proceed. Winter Owl led Eye of Crystal out, keeping a watchful eye on her, as if he was afraid she would speak out of turn again. Blade suspected that he might agree with Eye of Crystal if he knew more about this Challenge. He also knew that he couldn't say or do anything about it. The Guardian was going to do things his way and that was all there was to it.

The villagers who'd been inside the hut formed a ring around it, keeping the other villagers back at a safe distance. Two went and brought the Sweet Wisdom, in case either shaman's telepathy needed help. One of these was Winter Owl, and with him gone, Blade had a chance to talk to Crystal. He put down Moyla's body near Cheeky and led Crystal aside.

"What is this Challenge? A duel with the Voice?"

"Yes. They go together into the Sphere of Wisdom and fight with every weapon that may be used there."

Blade frowned. Even if he hadn't experienced Latan telepathy, he would have known this could be dangerous. There were too many Home Dimension tales of paranormal powers being used to kill; not all of them could be dimissed as nonsense.

"He did not have to do it," she said. She was as close to bursting into tears as Blade had ever seen her. "The Wise Bitch's life was his to take! But he knew the glory that came from the Challenge, and wanted it more than anything else!"

"It must be great glory, to make him want it so badly."

"It is. His name will live forever. But Blade, in the last three Challenges, all six of the Guardians and Wise Ones died."

"Damn," said Blade softly. It was inadequate, but then he himself felt just a little inadequate in the face of a man blithely going to his death so that his name would live forever. Perhaps the Guardian was not showing the highest degree of wisdom, but he was certainly showing a kind of courage Blade wondered if he had himself.

He put an arm around Eye of Crystal's shoulders, and a minute later Cheeky joined them.

("Is this Mistress a friend to the Master Blade?")

("Yes.")

("Then I want to be a friend to her.") Cheeky put one arm around Crystal's leg, barely reaching her knee. It might have looked silly, but Blade felt no urge to laugh. Cheeky was bearing up remarkably well after killing Moyla with his own hands. He shouldn't have had to learn about this dirty side of the spy business—the betrayal of friends—so soon.

Chapter 20

After all the furious preliminaries, the actual Challenge seemed almost tame, at least to Blade. After Winter Owl left the Sweet Wisdom in the hut and shut the door, the two Challengers might have gone to sleep for all anybody outside could tell.

"This is as it must be," said Crystal, seeing Blade's annoyance. "They go so far into the Sphere of Wisdom that anyone with a weak Voice could go mad in there with them."

"If they go so far and their Voices are so strong, isn't there danger of their Voices—leaking out?"

After a moment Crystal understood the image. "There is danger, that is all we know. Much danger. During the first of all Challenges, it is said that forty other people died or went mad. So this is not the time for you to learn more of the Voice. Would you put your hand into a fire to learn how hot it was?"

Blade shook his head. At least there was one consolation. No one in the village was allowed to use telepathy while the Challenge was being fought out. That eliminated the danger of some undiscovered enemy agent sending a warning to Ellspa. Such an agent might still be able to leave the village and warn her in person, but from Cheeky's account her hiding place was quite secluded. It would probably be daylight before they could find her. By then the warriors of the village would be scouring the countryside.

Blade also didn't mind not having anyone overhearing his thoughts, not even Cheeky. He was feeling more than a little angry with the world, Latan, and all the people in it, especially telepathic shamans with more courage than sense. Between them the Guardian and the Wise One probably knew the answers to every question about telepathy, including some he didn't know enough to ask. Now they were about to carry all their knowledge to the grave.

Blade knew that the two shamans had no obligation to him. He told himself that over and over again. It didn't help. He still wanted to pick up both shamans by the scruffs of their necks and bang their heads together until he'd pounded some sense into them.

In this mood, it was probably just as well he had no communication with Eye of Crystal. He doubted it would be very pleasant for her to learn what he was thinking about her father.

At least Winter Owl seemed to be having second thoughts about the Challenge. Perhaps he'd realized, now that it was too late, that the Guardian's glorious death was a very poor trade for the shaman's leadership in the war against the Rutari. The warrior paced up and down like a caged tiger, and when he thought no one was looking at him his face was twisted into a grim mask.

At last Winter Owl's pacing brought him close to Blade. "You took your life in your hands when you entered the *hiba-gan's* hut, I must tell you."

You can't show you've got nerves like the rest of us, thought Blade.

"That was not wisdom," Winter Owl went on. "Indeed, there may be some who doubt if you *have* wisdom. That is not a good thought, especially about a man with a Voice as strong as yours."

That is not a thought at all. It's just you fussing like an old woman.

"I had thought to take you among the warriors so that you might fight the Rutari beside us. Now, I do not know if that can be. Your slaying the *shpuga* and your skill at *nor* may not be the wisdom needed by a warrior of the Uchendi."

Blade swore under his breath. He'd been kept locked up among the Rutari because he was too valuable. Now he was likely to suffer the same fate among the Uchendi because he wouldn't kowtow to their bloody taboos!

"That must be as you wish, Winter Owl," Blade began, more calmly than he wanted to. But Eye of Crystal had overheard the conversation, her patience was gone, and now she had to confront her uncle.

"Mother's brother, you have already been as big a fool tonight as you should be. For the love of all who may think you better than a *shpuga*, do not try to be a bigger fool. You say that Blade has no wisdom and that you will keep him from the battles against the Rutari. Yet he had the wisdom to see what lay under the *hiba-gan's* cloak and defeat the Wise One. He might not have been her only victim, either. Would your Spirits call it well done if you and my father had both joined Blade in dying because he gave too much thought to laws made by fools and children?"

"Sister's daughter, you will be—"

"I will be nothing at your command, and never silent again!" She looked angry enough to strike her uncle. Blade moved so that he could step between them if the quarrel got that far out of hand.

"And you whine of keeping him out of the war, when he has made an English weapon that can slay *shpugas*! A weapon that can give us a sure victory over the Rutari! A weapon he will teach us to use, if you are not such a fool as to forbid him.

"You have nearly taken away our hopes of victory by letting my father do what he is doing. Blade can give us back our victory if you let him! If you do not, then I think the Spirits have forsaken you or perhaps the Rutari bought your—''

Winter Owl's hand went up and back, for a blow that would surely have knocked Crystal sprawling to the ground. Blade moved faster. His left hand shot out and clamped down on Winter Owl's wrist. His right hand dropped to the hilt of his knife. It took all his self-control not to break Winter Owl's arm or at least sink his free hand up to the wrist in the man's stomach.

Winter Owl was too surprised at Blade's intervention to resist or even shout. That gave Blade time to control his temper. When he finally spoke, only someone who knew him very well could have told he was in a rage.

''I will not judge your wisdom as you have judged mine, Winter Owl. I simply say that Eye of Crystal is telling the truth about the new weapon. I did not tell you about it because I wished to be sure that I could teach it to others.

''Now I know that I can. I will teach it to the warriors of the Uchendi, so they may kill the *shpugas* of the Rutari. I will teach it to all who will learn, whether you wish me to or not. The only way you can keep me from doing this is to kill me, and I will not lie down and be easy for you to kill.

''Now let us hold our tongues about this matter until the Challenge is over, or someone is sure to hear us and take up the quarrel. Both you and I are grown men and proven warriors. We do not need others telling us what to do.''

The threat of an open challenge to his authority and the reminder about other people listening seemed to calm Winter Owl. ''Very well,'' he said in a level voice. ''We shall be at peace with each other until the Challenge is past. Then you shall show me this weapon before you show it to anyone else.''

''That is good enough.'' Winter Owl hadn't asked for any oaths and Blade hadn't given any. As long as that was so, Blade could go ahead and show archery to anyone he wanted to afterward, whatever Winter Owl said.

And some people said life among primitive peoples was simple and free! Blade's experience led him to believe that taboo and custom and oath could snarl things up just as thoroughly as the most sophisticated civilized bureaucracy!

Blade released Winter Owl, and the warrior turned back to his niece with a look in his eyes Blade didn't like. If Winter Owl was going to work off his frustrations on Crystal, the whole bloody fight might have to be done over again! But whatever Winter Owl was going to say or do, he never got around to it. Suddenly a scream broke the silence and filled the darkness. It was a woman's scream, and there was both mental and physical agony in it—more agony than any one human being could ever stand.

The scream came again, then Blade heard faint moans and the sound of retching for a couple of minutes. At last silence returned, more complete than before, as everyone wondered what the screams meant but didn't dare to ask.

Blade cuddled Cheeky in the crook of one arm and put the other around Crystal. He would have embraced Winter Owl as well, if he'd thought the man needed that human comfort in the presence of the unknown.

After what seemed like hours but could only have been a few minutes, they heard the Guardian's voice calling from within the hut. It sounded almost frighteningly normal, but Blade noticed that Winter Owl drew his knife as he moved toward the door. Blade did the same, gave Cheeky to Eye of Crystal, and kept her behind him as they went in.

The Guardian was sitting slumped in a corner of the hut, a thin trickle of blood at one corner of his mouth. His eyes were open but seemed unfocused and wandering.

In the center of the hut lay the Wise One. Blade had never seen anyone who was more obviously dead, and few more gruesome corpses. The Wise One's face was contorted with awful pain, and in her last moment she'd emptied her bladder, bowels, and stomach. She'd even managed to dislocate some of her joints with the violence of her dying convulsions. The air was so thick with foul stenches that Blade felt even his iron stomach give one or two uncertain twitches, and Winter Owl clearly felt no better.

Crystal turned green and dashed for the fresh air. She stayed out only long enough to vomit herself empty, then returned with half a dozen reluctant warriors and women. By the time they'd carried out the Wise One's corpse and started scraping the floor of the hut, the Guardian was able to speak again.

"Daughter, wife's brother, B—Blade," he said. "The Wise One is dead. She fought hard in the Challenge, and honorably. Let her courage be remembered. . . ." His voice trailed off.

"For myself, I swear it," said Blade.

"I thought—English were honorable," said the Guardian. Then with a tremendous effort he focused his eyes and took in enough breath to speak steadily. "There is one more thing I must do tonight. I must read the poison on the dagger of the Wise One's First Friend. I took from her mind the picture of its being deadly, but not what it is. If we are to face it, we must know how to heal it."

Blade and Winter Owl looked at each other over Crystal's head. Before Blade could speak, Winter Owl nodded and said, "This will do more for the Uchendi than you think, sister's husband. Blade knows an English weapon that can hurl small spears the length of a village. It seems to be lawful, with no magic to it. If these—these—"

"Arrows," said Blade.

"If these arrows thrown by the bow were tipped with poison, what might they do to the *shpugas*?"

The Guardian managed a smile. "Nothing the Rutari will rejoice at, I think. And without their *shpugas*— Yes, it is true. I must read the poison at once, and be sure that someone else remembers what I learn. Then you who remain behind can make the poison, and my spirit will watch our victory if my body does not.''

"Father—'' began Eye of Crystal. She took a deep breath, crossed her hands over her breasts, and got herself under control. "Father, do you wish what I think you do?''

"Yes. I will cause the poison to enter my body, and you will join me in the Sphere of Wisdom while it does its work. Remember what I say and what you see as I taught you, and you will be able to make the poison as easily as the Wise One.''

"Father, I know I must help in the reading. I have the healing knowledge more than anyone else here. But must—must it be *you*?''

"I am dying, daughter. Indeed, I have been dying since the spring. My heart has been failing. I knew that I would be of little use next year, so I chose to die by the Challenge.''

No one said anything. They all seemed to realize there was nothing to say. The Guardian smiled. "Come, daughter. Be true to all I have taught you. I cannot condemn anyone to die by the poison just to spare your heart. The only condemned man in the village now is River Over Stones. Would you choose to spend time in his mind?''

Crystal shuddered at the idea. "His mind is like a nest of snakes at best. It will be even worse tonight. Also, he does not have the Voice so strongly. He might not be able to tell me what must be known, even if he wished to.''

"Which he will not," said the Guardian. "Do you know what must be done?''

"Yes.'' Crystal stood, blinking back the tears for a moment, then motioned to the others. "Leave us, please.''

Blade obeyed so quickly he almost felt guilty. He would have given a lot to stand by Crystal in her coming ordeal. What made it worse was that she'd brought it on herself.

If she hadn't revealed the archery to Winter Owl, he would never have spoken to the Guardian. If the Guardian hadn't known about archery, he would never have insisted on this painful method of reading the poison.

But if the poison wasn't analyzed the Uchendi would lost a major weapon against their enemies. And this after losing the Guardian's telepathic skills and leadership!

As usual, there was no easy solution.

Blade had long since become reconciled to this fact of life. He still hadn't managed to get used to seeing people like Eye of Crystal ground to mincemeat by the machinery of a badly run universe.

Chapter 21

The Guardian died at dawn. Eye of Crystal managed to gasp out how to make the poison, then collapsed so completely that Blade was afraid she was dying, too.

Her mother assured him this was probably not so. "She would spare herself no more than her father," Kyarta said quietly, "but this is most likely no more than a sleep that will heal her if she is left in it. I will watch over her to be sure that it is nothing worse. You and Winter Owl will be the first called if I need anyone."

Then, dry eyed, she gave orders for litter-bearers to carry away her unconscious daughter to their hut and her dead husband to the Dead House. There he would be embalmed with herbs and ashes. After lying for a month he would be cremated at the Burning Stairs by the river.

Kyarta, who Blade wouldn't have been surprised to see fall completely apart, seemed to be taking things calmly. Blade was glad to have someone else watch over Eye of Crystal. He and Winter Owl already had enough to do without that.

Warriors had to go find Ellspa's hiding place and if possible Ellspa herself. Cheeky gave the best directions he could, but no one could follow his route through the treetops. It was three days before they found the ruined hut. By that time the bird had flown so long ago that Winter Owl didn't even try to pick up her trail.

"I'd rather have bagged her along with her Mistress,"
Blade reassured the chief. "But I don't think she'll do
much harm. She won't be able to learn about the archery
and warn the Rutari."

"Perhaps not," said Winter Owl. "But I think it would
be best if the men we are teaching the archery were to go
to a new camp. No one except those men will be allowed in
it, or even near it. If Ellspa is hiding somewhere in Uchendi
lands or if the Rutari have other spies, this will keep them
from learning what they should not know."

"Good idea," said Blade. In fact, Winter Owl seemed
to have got a firm grip on himself. He'd stopped arguing
with Blade and even refused to quarrel with his niece. His
brother-in-law's death and the knowledge that the war
with the Rutari was fast approaching had sobered him.
Blade no longer worried about Winter Owl's turning the
warriors of the Uchendi against him or his new ideas.

In fact, Winter Owl worked nonstop for a week to get
the Uchendi archers off to a good start, taking time off
only for food and sleep and not much of either. By the end
of the week he'd picked a hundred men to learn to shoot
and fifty craftsmen to make bows, bowstrings, and
arrows. Blade helped choose the wood for the bows and
arrows.

"With the poison, the small reed arrows I used may be
enough," he said. "But we have not made any of the
poison yet, let alone tested it to make sure it is strong
enough. So we must be ready to make arrows strong
enough to hurt a *shpuga* without the poison.

"Also, when the *shpugas* are all dead and the Rutari are
defeated, you will be using the arrows to hunt birds and
animals. We do not know if the poison will make them bad
to eat. Again, you will need strong arrows so that your
children may have full bellies."

The warriors looked at him, trusting but obviously confused. Without any telepathy, Blade could tell what they

were thinking: *Is he mad, to be so sure of victory over the Rutari?*

Blade wasn't mad. He wasn't even overly confident, at least by his own standards. He simply had a piece of knowledge no one else among the Rutari or the Uchendi had, and he had no intention of sharing it with anyone right now.

He knew where the Rutari had hidden the stolen Idol.

Blade learned this from Cheeky, which was one reason he couldn't talk about his discovery. The Uchendi were still a little suspicious of Cheeky. Of the two people who might have trusted him, the Guardian was dead and his daughter sick. Blade couldn't help noticing the number of people making motions to avert evil Spirits when they saw Cheeky.

Blade saw even more gestures than usual the morning he and Cheeky buried Moyla. Blade dug the hole and laid her in it, then shoveled the earth back. Cheeky mourned with a high-pitched wail that set Blade's teeth on edge, then piled stones on the grave until there was a little cairn. As they walked back to the village, Blade saw people not only making gestures of aversion but actually stepping out of their path.

Apart from the burial, Cheeky didn't spend much time mourning for Moyla. ("She wished too much bad for Master Blade, friends of Master Blade. I wish she was not dead. But I will not be weak about it. Mistress Crystal is strong about the death of her father, who did not wish any bad to anyone. I must be strong about the death of Moyla. I wish Mistress Crystal to be my friend.")

("I think she will be, Cheeky.")

("That will make me happy.")

With Cheeky showing that kind of courage, Blade didn't really care who thought he was an evil Spirit. The little fellow was back. He also gave enough information about the Rutari to lay to rest any last doubts in Blade's mind about where his loyalties really lay.

Blade was impressed by the intelligence Cheeky had

shown in using his relationship with Moyla and Ellspa to spy on the Rutari. ("You keep this up, little friend, and J will want to hire *you* as an agent.")

("I do not want to work for the Master J.")

("You do not like him?")

("He is a good man, and he is your friend. But he is not you. I do not want to have to obey too many Masters I do not know.")

("Sensible.") Then as an afterthought: ("Will you do what the Master Leighton tells you?")

("He is not such a good man. Why should I do what he tells me?")

("You want to learn more about your strong thoughts?")

("Yes.")

("Leighton can teach you more about them than anybody else, if you will do what he wants.")

("I will think about it.")

That was as much of a promise as Blade could get out of Cheeky. He was pleasantly surprised to get even that much. The increase in Cheeky's intelligence was apparently permanent; he hadn't taken a dose of *kerush* since he came south with Ellspa, but his strong thoughts were coming just as smoothly. By the time they got back to Home Dimension, there'd be even less justification than before to treat Cheeky like a laboratory animal.

Not to mention the fact that Cheeky would hardly put up with such treatment. His main experience with scientific research was in the Dimension of Kaldak, with the Seekers of Doimar. Their cruelty was not exactly good promotion for scientific research. Blade wouldn't have blamed Cheeky if he'd refused to ever see the inside of a laboratory again.

After the second week in their camp the archers seemed to be making progress, or at least able to hit something smaller than a large hut. The craftsmen could make bows and strings that wouldn't snap on the first pull, and arrows that sometimes flew almost straight.

Even the Healers trying to brew up the poison were making progress. The main ingredient was the crushed seeds of a marsh plant that grew only in a few places. They'd had to make a long trip to bring back enough for their experiments, and they'd have to make an even longer one to get enough to make poison for the war.

Blade hoped the Rutari would give them at least enough time to carry out his plan. However, he himself wasn't going to do anything to slow down the coming of the war. In fact, he told the Uchendi that he intended to make sure it would happen as soon as possible, at a place of the Uchendi's own choosing.

"Or as close to it as you can hope for in war," he added.

"We are not ignorant of war," said Winter Owl. Kyarta and the recovering Eye of Crystal nodded. "We know you hope for much. Now tell me how this is to be done."

"I will go north and bring back the Idol," he said. "The Rutari will immediately march south to bring it back. We will wait for them."

Three sets of open mouths and wide eyes greeted that statement. It was Kyarta who came to first.

"You know where the Idol is?"

"Yes. Cheeky told me." He scratched the feather-monkey's crest. "He learned it from the Wise One and Ellspa. In fact, he stayed behind to learn this because he knew I wanted to know. I did not know that this was his reason for staying with the Rutari, so I was angry with him. Now I know that he may have saved the Uchendi."

Nobody here knew about Cheeky's relations with Moyla, except possibly Crystal. Blade was quite happy to keep it that way. He also didn't bother telling them that Cheeky had actually gone to see the Idol with the two shamans of the Rutari. Nobody would believe that.

Winter Owl was nodding. "It is indeed best to make your enemy come to you. We would have to send many warriors north to beat the Rutari. While they were away the Rutari might come south and attack the women and children in the villages.'' Winter Owl's expression said the rest to anyone who hadn't seen the Rutari dealing with enemy prisoners.

"But—is the Cheeky trustworthy? I do not doubt that he is lawful, Blade. If he was not, he could not have lived around you as he has. But does he know as much as he thinks he does?''

Blade felt Cheeky stiffen and start to bristle under his hand. Some of Winter Owl's doubts must be reaching him telepathically. Blade stroked Cheeky and spoke more sharply to the warrior than he would have over an insult to himself.

"I have trusted my life to Cheeky many times, and I am still alive. Do you doubt my word on this?''

Winter Owl did not, and said so. But he still looked worried, and Crystal noticed it. "Blade,'' she asked, "might I come with you to seek the Idol?''

Both her mother and her uncle stared and started to protest. She raised her voice sharply. "I can watch over the Cheeky to see if he is leading us astray. I can also guard Blade's back, for I have eyes and ears if no great war skill, although I can carry a bow and hunt with it.''

She lowered her voice. "Also, I am the daughter of the Guardian, gifted with the Voice. I am not stronger than Blade, but I know that I or someone like me should be present when the Uchendi take back the Idol. It might be angry otherwise.''

Kyarta nodded slowly. She was clearly torn between reluctance to risk her daughter after losing her husband and knowing the girl was telling the truth. Loyalty to her tribe won out. "Yes. You will know the ways of the Idol better than Blade. His Voice is strong but it is not ours.''

"I have no weak Voice,'' said Winter Owl. "Also, I am a proven warrior. I think it would be better for me to go.''

Blade shook his head. "One of us has to stay behind and

train the warriors in archery. Plus, you could not speak as well as I to the Cheeky, who knows where the Idol is to be found. That means it must be I who goes north. Also, if the warriors are properly trained, the Uchendi will have their victory whether or not I come back. We must think of that as well.''

Nobody was foolish enough to ignore that idea. Winter Owl had to agree with Blade, and started talking of what Blade and Eye of Crystal would need on their trip.

Afterward, Crystal pulled Blade aside into a doorway and kissed him with surprising warmth. ''You have done more for me than I could tell you with Winter Owl listening,'' she whispered. ''One who becomes the Guardian must pass a Warrior's Test. That is why no woman has ever been a Guardian.''

After a moment Blade realized what she meant. ''Then—our trip north will be your Test?''

''It can be, if you will bear witness that I have done as a warrior should.''

She was obviously dead serious. Blade put an arm around her and said, ''I will.''

''Bless you.''

Blade wasn't sure it deserved a blessing. Did Crystal know what she might be getting into, going against so many customs and taboos? Probably not. On the other hand, it was her life and her people. If she wanted to succeed her father and become the first female Guardian, why not help her?

Chapter 22

("Is that it?") Blade asked, pointing to the mouth of the cave.

Perched on Blade's shoulder, Cheeky said "Yes" by tugging twice on Blade's right ear.

So their journey to the Idol was over. Now all that remained was to get down the rocky slope below them into the mist-hung valley, enter the cave, find the Idol, and get themselves and it safely out of reach of the Rutari.

If you were a comic-book superhero, easy enough. But if you were a comic-book superhero, you didn't have to spend ten days of foot-bruising, muscle-wrenching hiking just getting this far. Your stomach didn't rumble when you hadn't found any game for two days, and you didn't pick up more bruises ducking for cover to avoid Rutari patrols—or rolling on the ground with an enthusiastic young lady.

As Blade watched, the mist thinned for a moment. He could see farther back into the cave. He could also see two men sitting by a small fire in the lee of boulders just beyond the cave mouth. Both wore loinguards and had their spears propped against a boulder. They didn't look alert, but their presence was still a problem.

("Were there men with spears here when you came with Ellspa and the Wise One?")

After a moment's hesitation, Cheeky tugged Blade's ear once for "No."

So Ellspa or at least a message from her had reached home. Now the Rutari knew things weren't going quite the way the Wise One had planned. Or perhaps Ellspa herself was visiting the Idol?

("Can you hear any of the thoughts of the Mistress Ellspa?")

Cheeky was silent for so long that before he replied the mist blotted out the mouth of the cave and the sentries. Then he gave the "No" tug.

That didn't prove that Ellspa wasn't present; she might be asleep or making love. At least she didn't seem to be in *kerush-magor* or some other state of telepathic sensitivity where she might pick up Blade's thoughts no matter how he tried to conceal them.

Telepathy, Blade realized now, had a good deal in common with radio. For example, when you broadcast, you had to be sure you had some chance of telling if the enemy was alert and likely to intercept you. For Blade, it made it easier to understand telepathy to be able to compare it to something he already knew.

So on the way north, Blade and Crystal had been able to work out security precautions, and Cheeky was cooperating nicely. The two humans would use no telepathy at all to each other. They would use it as seldom as possible to Cheeky. When they did use it, he would answer whenever possible with ear-tugs for "Yes" or "No." Blade hoped this would produce the telepathic equivalent of radio silence. He would have been more careful with the Wise One and Moyla still alive, and not used any telepathic communications. Against Rutari, dependent as far as he knew either on Ellspa or *kerush-magor*, the limited telepathy should be safe.

Blade mentally crossed his fingers and looked down at the sentry post again. He could see one man coming out of the cave with an armload of firewood. This lack of alertness was encouraging. It was hard to believe that Ellspa or any warrior who knew his business would allow it.

"I don't think Ellspa is here, or any other strong leader," he said to Crystal. "Do you know why?" He was testing her knowledge of war.

She gave him the same reasons he'd already considered, then added, "There may be more back in the cave. But if we move fast, we will be able to kill the two outside before the others can help them. Then we can wait for them to come out and be killed."

"Perhaps," said Blade. "It would be better if we killed the two outside so fast that they give no warning. Others inside might hide the Idol, or even take it out another way. Are you sure there is only one mouth to this cave?"

Crystal looked annoyed with herself, then shook her head. Blade patted her shoulder. "Never mind. You thought like a warrior, and I will swear this before all the Uchendi. Some things that you must know, you will learn only with experience. Winter Owl did not know everything either when he was your age."

There was still one problem. Blade wouldn't have a good shot with his bow unless the sentries could be lured out into the open. With better arrows or the crossbow, he would have risked picking them off in their shelter of boulders, but with the weapons he had it was necessary to make other plans.

He explained those plans to Crystal while he strung the bow and checked the feathers on his arrows for damage from the wet weather. He had a dozen of the best wooden arrows the Uchendi could make; that should be enough against two surprised men who would never have heard of archery.

Crystal listened wide eyed, trying to stifle giggles. Then she crept behind the nearest boulder and stripped naked. She went on giggling as she did so, and Blade hoped she didn't think this whole thing was a game. There wasn't much he could do or say if she did, though—not with her whims of steel!

With Cheeky on her back and clinging to her hair, Crystal crept off down the slope on hands and knees. Blade did the same, moving off at a sharp angle. By the time he reached the floor of the valley, Crystal was already in place. She sent him a brief mental picture of what she could see from where she was, and Blade had to admit she'd chosen the place well.

("Good thinking. But don't go into your act until I tell you.")

Blade lay still for another minute, to make sure the telepathic communication hadn't alerted the sentries. Then he crept forward to the boulder he'd picked. It was big enough to hide him while he stood and drew his bow, and around it was clear ground to give him good footing while he shot. Blade picked his best arrow, nocked it to the bow, and sent his message to Crystal.

("Now!")

Fifty yards up the slope from the mouth of the cave, a dark-haired figure rose into sight. The sentries looked up and saw a naked woman standing there watching them. Perched on her shoulder was an animal. They looked again, and Blade could almost read their thoughts without telepathy, from the looks on their faces. Then:

"Wise One! You didn't die!" one of them shouted. "Blessings for that!"

"No blessings for lazy swine like you!" shouted Crystal, pitching her voice as low as possible. The two guards looked at each other. "Is this her or—?" one of them said, afraid to follow his own thoughts to their conclusion.

The other threw up his hands in despair. "Spirit or flesh, she summons us. I will go, if you are afraid."

"If she allows, I will have your blood for those words," the second man growled. Then they both did exactly what Blade wanted them to do, stepping out onto the open slope away from the boulders.

"No, *I* will have your blood," said Blade, only half to himself. He took two steps to the left and shot his first arrow. It flew wide, but the two Rutari had no ears or eyes for anything except the apparition of the Wise One. Blade had plenty of time to shoot again. The second arrow hit the first sentry in the thigh.

He let out a scream that echoed around the valley. Crystal shuddered visibly, but the second man didn't notice. He looked wildly around and apparently decided the scream was from the Wise One. Now that he was satisfied that she had returned as an evil Spirit to curse him, no amount of respect for her memory could keep him at his post. Without a backward glance at spear or comrade, he took to his heels.

Blade nocked a third arrow with flying fingers. Not far beyond the running man was more rough ground. If he got into that he'd be so hard to hit that he would have a good chance of getting away. His tale of what happened might not be accurate, but it would damned sure bring more Rutari warriors up here in a hurry! Blade thought he and Crystal could do better without this.

Blade could also have done without Crystal's idea of help. As he aimed for the running man, she ran down the slope, her knife in her hand and Cheeky clinging desperately to her hair. Screaming like a real Spirit, she leaped on the staggering wounded man and slammed him to the rocky ground. Blade didn't dare shoot for fear of hitting her, and by the time he was able to let fly, the running man was no easy shot.

The arrow drew another scream. Blade dropped his bow, snatched up his spear, then dashed forward. He hoped he hadn't hit Crystal and was determined to teach her a lesson if he hadn't.

Crystal was covered with blood when Blade reached her, but she was grinning with such savage delight that he knew it must be her victim's. He dashed on past her until the second sentry appeared out of the mist. He was stumbling along, the arrow in his back, one hand groping behind him for the source of this mysterious pain. Hearing Blade coming up behind him, he turned just in time to take Blade's spear in his chest.

When he was sure the second man was dead, Blade returned to Crystal. She was wiping her knife off on the dead man's hair, and wiping herself off with a bunch of dead grass. As Blade approached she jumped up and threw her arms around him. It was a much more enthusiastic embrace than Blade enjoyed receiving from a naked young woman when he couldn't do anything about it.

"That's two for my father's Spirit. Two, and they won't be the last!" she crowed.

"It might have been only one, and us in danger," growled Blade. "You must understand the way of weapons like my bow. Never, never, *never* get in their path when I am using them. An arrow flying a long way cannot always tell a friend from an enemy. *You* might have had an arrow here—" he patted her flat stomach "—instead of the two sentries."

Instead of being apologetic, Crystal wriggled with pleasure under his touch. Danger and vengeance for her father seemed to be working on her like a love potion.

Blade sighed. "Crystal, if you try to draw me into making love to you now, I shall turn you over my knee and spank you. There is much to be done before we can safely do that. Have you forgotten why we came?"

She pressed her face into his chest. "Am I no longer desirable to you?"

He put his arms around her. "You are even more desirable than ever." This was the simple truth. She'd lost weight on their trek north, without losing her magnificent figure. "Left to myself, I would have you down on the ground—"

"Not on the ground, please, Blade. The stones would be hard. On our cloaks, at least."

Blade laughed. "On our cloaks. But as I said, we are not

our own masters. There is the Idol close by, ready for us. Who knows? It might make me impotent, if we tried to make love before we rescued it from the unlawful hands of the Rutari!''

Eye of Crystal looked horror-struck, whether at the idea of the Idol's wrath or Blade's impotence was hard to tell. Then she looked up toward the mouth of the cave and nodded.

''Let us go and seek the Idol, then. Once we have it, perhaps its magic will make you stronger.''

''Woman, you've got a one-track mind,'' said Blade, patting her rump as she started up the slope ahead of him.

Blade would have been happier if he'd known exactly what they were looking for. Knowing where the Idol was hadn't answered the question of exactly *what* it was.

No living man among the Uchendi had seen the Idol. The Rutari carried it off something like eighty years ago. Cheeky had seen it, but only from a distance, in poor light, and while he was desperately trying to hide the fact that he was looking at it from the Wise One, Ellspa, and Moyla.

Somehow Blade pieced together enough information to keep his job from being completely hopeless. The Idol was made of metal harder than any the tribes knew and worked in ways they could not understand. It was small enough that one person could carry it—Cheeky had seen Ellspa do so.

That was all he knew. In a way it made the mystery of the Idol greater and more tantalizing than ever. Now at last Blade was at the mouth of the Idol's cave, with no one to stop him from going in. According to Cheeky's memories, the Idol lay about three hundred feet inside the darkness.

Blade's feet were itching to carry him into the cave, but he controlled them. While he covered her with the bow, Crystal retrieved their packs. She returned wearing trousers and sandals again, with some of her lightheadedness gone. Taking vengeance for her father with her own hands must have been a tonic to her, but Blade was glad it was wearing off. It was a long way home.

In the packs were four torches made of reeds dipped in animal fat, then bound tightly around wooden sticks. Blade took out two torches and blew up the sentries' abandoned fire until some embers were glowing again. It was smoking like the devil, but with the mist swirling around so thickly Blade wasn't worried about anyone noticing the smoke. Thrust into the embers, the torches began to smoke, then burn, then shed a flickering, sickly yellow light.

Just enough to keep us from falling down holes, thought Blade, and to Cheeky, (''All right, little friend. Lead on.'') Aloud, he told Crystal, ''Stay behind me and keep a lookout toward the mouth of the cave.'' There was no point in leaving her alone on guard at the entrance; she'd be in more danger and Blade would be in no less.

Slowly Cheeky walked along the damp rock to the mouth of the cave, then waited for Blade and Crystal to come up behind him. He moved on, to the limits of the torchlight, then *yeeped* plaintively. His unhappiness at being so close to the darkness was obvious. Blade took three steps forward while Crystal stayed where she was, extending the light of his torch that much farther into the cave. Cheeky *yeeeped* again, this time happily, and hopped forward. . . .

Chapter 23

Blade quickly lost track of time as they moved in this leapfrog fashion deeper into the darkness of the Idol's cave. As they moved, Crystal laid out a fine leather thong dyed white, marking their path back to the outside world. She carried only three hundred feet of it. If Cheeky's estimate of the distance to the Idol was badly off, they'd face an interesting choice: abandon the search or risk going on into the darkness beyond the end of the thong.

They groped their way through the cave, their hands feeling what their eyes couldn't see in the flickering light of the torches. It seemed to Blade that the walls and ceiling of the cave had been untouched by anything but dripping water and stagnant air since before man existed. The slimy dark rock around them seemed to be closing in on them, narrowing down until it was only a little higher than Blade and barely wide enough for him and Crystal to stand side by side. Blade noticed that the thong was about half gone.

("Is this—the way you remember?")

("Oh, yes," said Cheeky blithely. "We do not have far to go.")

Now the tunnel was sloping downhill and beginning to curve slightly to the left. Cheeky started *yeeping* excitedly. Blade signaled to Crystal to come up close behind him, handed her the other torch, and drew his knife. It would be a more useful weapon at close quarters than either spear or bow.

"If we are attacked," he said over his shoulder, "grab Cheeky and run! No point in both of us getting killed."

There was no sound from Crystal except a small defiant snort. She obviously had her own opinion about abandoning Blade, but there was no time to argue. Twenty feet more and the tunnel opened up to a larger cave.

"Raise those torches high," Blade said, and stepped forward.

In the center of the chamber was a pile of black stones and ashes, the remains of a fire. Behind that was an altar of mountain stone roughly mortared together. On the altar lay the Idol. It gleamed metallically, and there was something oddly familiar about the shape. . . .

Blade's feet carried him halfway across the cave before he realized what the Idol was. The moment of recognition brought him to a stop so sharply that he swayed, and both Cheeky and Crystal cried out in alarm and reached for him. He waved them to silence and stared intently at the Idol, trying to convince his brain that his eyes were telling the truth.

On the altar lay an UZI submachine gun, a perfectly ordinary piece of Home Dimension weaponry. There was one forty-round magazine in the gun, and three more magazines of 9mm rounds arranged in a little tripod to one side.

Somebody in Home Dimension must have traveled into this land of Latan—who? and how long ago? No one could recall precisely how long the Idol had been in Uchendi hands before the Rutari stole it eighty years ago, but it had to be at least a century. So this UZI had been in Latan for nearly two hundred years.

Or at least two hundred years as this Dimension measured time. Blade knew that didn't necessarily mean much—the Project had discovered some time ago that time in one Dimension wasn't always related to time in any other. On his second trip to Kaldak, Blade found that his daughter, who hadn't been born when he left the first time, was now about thirty years old! Also, he'd once left a Dimension where he was about to be burned at the stake and then returned only second later, after weeks in another Dimension. Project Dimension X might tell them some very important things about the nature of time. The only problem was, once again, knowing what questions to ask.

A more immediate problem was examining this UZI: UZIs were found all over the world, and this one might well have been stripped of any markings telling where it originated. But if he could just get it back Home and have J's weapons experts go over it—and he'd better keep that thought to himself. . . .

He stepped up to the altar and picked up the Idol. The UZI hadn't been stripped of its markings; it had a serial number and some ordnance department's markings on it in the usual places. Blade raised the UZI to get a closer look—and this time it seemed as if the chamber and even reality itself were swaying around him.

The UZI bore the markings of the Ordnance Corps of the Imperial and Royal Army of Englor.

Englor. The alternate England fighting against the Red Flames of Russland. Their army used UZIs—one of the many bizarre parallels between Englor's Dimension and Home Dimension. This was a UZI that had somehow made its way from Englor's Dimension to the Dimension of the tribal warriors of Latan.

At least Blade found that explanation more agreeable than the idea that he'd gone completely mad and the UZI, the cave of the Idol, and God knows what else was an elaborate hallucination. He did not want to wake up strapped to a bed in the mental ward of a secret hospital. He'd been through that before with the Ngaa, and once was too often.

Some of the other men from Home Dimension who'd

tried traveling into Dimension X were still in such wards. They'd be there for life, too, their hold on *any* reality snapped forever by exposure to an alternate one.

No, he would act on the assumption that he was really holding an Englor army-issue UZI submachine gun, and consider how it could have got here. It seemed to Blade that there were three ways.

Latan could be on the same alternate Earth as Englor, Russland, Gallia, and so on.

Latan could be on another planet in the same Dimension as Englor, which had developed spaceflight and reached it.

Englor had discovered the Dimension X secret on its own and had left the gun in Latan. This last possibility —that Englor had discovered inter-Dimension travel— was the most unpleasant. It also seemed to Blade the most likely.

If the Englorians were on the same planet, it was possible that they should not have come to Latan again some time in the last two hundred years. Or it was impossible unless there'd been a war large enough to destroy civilization and leave remote parts of the planet isolated. That didn't seem likely. Such a war would certainly have affected the whole planet violently enough for there to be legends about it. Blade hadn't heard anything of the kind.

An interplanetary expedition also seemed unlikely. There were no legends of the Idol Makers coming out of the sky. One day they hadn't been there, the next day they had. After a while another day came when they were simply gone, leaving the Idol behind.

No, Englor had discovered Dimension X and sent at least one full-scale expedition into it. (Never mind whether there was more than one Englor. That way lay madness.) The Englorians had left the gun here, the inhabitants of Latan had found it, and they had made it into an Idol. That seemed the best explanation for everything Blade had seen here. He remembered with uneasy clarity

Lord Leighton's words about the Dimension X secret probably not really being much of a secret anymore.

And if Englor discovered inter-Dimensional travel at least two centuries ago, what had they done with it since then? Except that it might not be two centuries to Englor's Dimension; it might be only a few years.

There were too bloody many questions running around loose for Blade's peace of mind. He decided to start reducing them as fast as he could. Step one was to pick up the Idol and the magazines and stow them away in his pack. Step two was to get back outside.

Step three was to get out of Rutari territory as fast as possible. Blade knew he just might find a few answers by exploring these caves, but it was likely that somebody would notice the missing sentries, draw the appropriate conclusions, and make more trouble than he and Crystal and Cheeky could handle.

Blade scooped the magazines into his pack and picked up the gun. The UZI's plastic sling was cracked and yellow with age and spotted with mold. Blade unhooked it and left it on the altar, making a mental note to make a new sling out of some of the leather thong once they were out of the cave. A sling would leave both hands free for a use-able weapon like his bow and arrow. He couldn't imagine that the UZI was still useable, and even if it wasn't a piece of junk, the ammunition would have deteriorated hopelessly.

Blade grabbed Crystal and said, "We have the Idol. Let us take it to its lawful home among your people before the Rutari come."

Crystal nodded and found the leather thong. They followed the thong back to the entrance of the cave. Outside they delayed their leaving just long enough for Blade to find a deep crevice in the side of the valley. He dropped the two dead sentries and all their gear down the crevice. It was now getting toward the rainy season in this part of the mountains; one good storm would wash away any bloodstains. If it looked as if the sentries had vanished by magic, it might sow fear among the Rutari and delay their pursuit, giving the Uchendi more time to prepare for the attack.

With Cheeky on Blade's back, he and Eye of Crystal walked hand and hand into the mist as the valley of the Idol vanished behind them.

Chapter 24

They were in Uchendi territory, as far as Blade and Crystal could remember. They'd been in it since dawn, and both now looked forward to a good night's sleep with no worries about mounting guard. Cheeky shared their pleasure, though Crystal had been heard to grumble that he hadn't shared the sentry duty. Although there had been no physical or telepathic signs of pursuit, they still couldn't take chances.

"It would be just too shameful for us to end up spitted by some *ezinti* herder either of us could have slain with one hand," Crystal said. "I will not go into the Great Sleep merely to gain more of the Little Sleep."

Very sharp indeed, thought Blade. Eye of Crystal had enough common sense about war, apart from what he was teaching her, to make a good war chief. Of course they weren't going to let her take that job, but this wisdom might ease her way to becoming She Who Guards the Voice. She'd have to play that one herself, though. He wasn't likely to be around to advise her.

Now it looked as if they might not be able to sleep easy tonight after all. There were too many small signs of a large mounted party in the area—*ezinti* droppings and a few tracks, traces of campfires and latrines imperfectly hidden.

"Maybe it is Uchendi," said Eye of Crystal.

"Maybe," said Blade. "But then why would they be trying to hide at all?" Both tribes were careful about leaving clean campsites; they were natural ecologists. But neither spent the extra time involved in concealing all their traces when they were in friendly territory.

"You think the enemy is ahead of us?"

"I think we should be ready for the worst."

Blade debated with himself the idea of burying the Idol, then the two of them splitting up and heading south separately. One of them should make it home and be able to lead the Uchendi back to the person with the Idol. However, the Rutari might already be watching them. Besides, he was reluctant to leave Crystal, and she would almost certainly refuse to leave him.

They moved on, eyes roaming the landscape, hands close to weapons. Blade had his bow strung and wished that he had a functional UZI or even a good automatic pistol with an extra magazine. . . .

They came up to the bank of a stream, and Blade looked carefully up and down it, then at the hillside above the far bank. Lots of rocks and stunted trees, but nothing within spear-throw. He motioned Eye of Crystal forward after him. As she came she unslung their waterskins from her belt and dipped them into the stream.

Blade stepped up onto the far bank. Crystal was reslinging the bulging waterskins when suddenly the hillside sprouted human figures. Blade froze, then grabbed wildly for his bow, turned to shout to Eye of Crystal—then recognized the figures as Uchendi archers, raising and drawing their bows. Only one actually let fly, but that arrow went *thuk* into the gravel bank no more than a yard from Blade. He pulled it out and waved it at the archers, not sure whether he should curse them for their taste in practical jokes or praise them for their skill in laying the ambush. If all those archers had let fly, he and Crystal and Cheeky would now be punctured corpses turning the stream pink.

Cheeky was *yeeeping* with the tone Blade recognized as his laughter.

("All right, you little bugger, what's so funny?")

("You are, Master. I felt you getting ready to die, when I knew the Masters on the hill were friends.")

("You—you heard their minds?") For a moment Blade felt like dunking the feather-monkey in the stream to improve his manners.

("Yes. I am sorry if it was a wrong thing. I would have told you if I heard the minds of the bad Rutari Masters.")

("I should bloody well hope so!") Cheeky might be more intelligent now, but he was still an incorrigible practical joker. Blade shuddered at the thought of the feather-monkey's getting in telepathic contact with the Project's computer—then realized that under controlled conditions that might be a rather valuable experiment.

Meanwhile, the Uchendi warriors were running down the hillside toward Blade and Crystal, laughing and shouting their war cries. They ran up to Blade, each boasting about his skill in finding a hiding place. Several of the archers got into a lively argument over whether they should have been the one to shoot the arrow, and if they had whether they would have done better than Friend of Lions. They all expected Blade to praise them. He would have been perfectly happy to do so if he'd been able to get a word in!

Blade waited until the warriors started running out of breath and Winter Owl came down the bank. Then he said, "You have learned well what you must know, it seems to me."

"It was Winter Owl's doing more than any others," said Friend of Lions. "He said that we should learn to shoot from hiding and far away, so the poison would have time to work in the *shpugas*. A dying *shpuga* is as deadly as an unhurt one. The only *shpuga* it is safe to have close to you is a dead one."

"Even better, a rotten one," said someone.

"Well, they will all be rotting soon enough," said Winter Owl. "And we will put their heads on the Guardian's grave, so his Spirit will know that we have finished his work."

That got a chorus of agreement. Obviously Friend of Lions and Winter Owl were now getting along famously. While the warriors started talking again, Blade unslung his pack and opened it. As they saw what he was doing, the warriors seemed to realize what was coming. One by one they fell silent. By the time Blade raised the Idol over his head, the silence was like a graveyard's.

It lasted a long time. Even Eye of Crystal got down on her knees and closed her eyes, although she'd seen the Idol morning, noon, and night since they left the cave. She wasn't the only one closing her eyes, either. Half the warriors seemed to be afraid that if they looked at the Idol it would vanish. Were they dreaming or was Blade doing some magic to make them believe that they saw what was not there?

Winter Owl kept his eyes open, and it was finally his voice that broke the silence. "Rise up and look, Uchendi. *It is the Idol returned!*"

Then everyone was cheering and shouting, crowding around Blade and Eye of Crystal, almost ready to lift them up and carry them around. Cheeky was scared half out of his wits; he *yeeeped* frantically and burrowed out of sight in Blade's pack. Between the heads of the warriors Blade saw Crystal laughing and kissing every warrior who offered himself. For the first time since her father's death, Blade no longer saw his ghost in her eyes.

This was a victory, his first real one in this Dimension. But it was only one victory. They still had to win the war.

Teindo idly stroked Ellspa's bare thigh. It and the rest of her glistened in the firelight with love sweat. Teindo himself felt his hair matted and damp from their exertions.

It had been some time since he was with a woman so eager and so young.

However, his wits were not tired. Even if they had been, he would still have spoken out. To do otherwise would be to betray the warriors of the Rutari. There had been enough betrayal already, without his adding more.

"Is it still your command that we ride at once into the south, to seek the Idol?"

Ellspa sat up. Although she still looked splendid, she was clearly angry.

"Did you think that bedding me would make me change my mind? I did not worship a man's weapon even when I was an unbroached girl. Now I am the Wise One of the Rutari."

"Between us you are. The lawful rites have not taken place. And who knows what other rites may be needed, with the Wise One dying as she did?"

"And how long will all of these rites take?"

"I am not—"

"Teindo, you are not an adept in the *kerush-magor*. Therefore how can you know anything of these matters?"

"Perhaps I cannot. But you cannot be the Wise One simply by saying so."

"Then let the war against the Uchendi begin without our having a Wise One. I shall go and do what I can, and we will think of rites when the Idol is returned."

Teindo closed his eyes. The idea appalled him. Ellspa slapped him across the cheek, lightly, to get his attention, but in a way that told him clearly she was in a rage and not to be trifled with.

"Teindo, what purpose would there be in war, if the lawless have time to hide the Idol or even destroy it?"

"We do not know what new war-magic the Englishman Blade may have taught them. The Idol will not save our warriors if they cannot face his magic."

"You think a warrior of the English has greater power than the Idol?"

"The Idol allowed him to take it back to the Uchendi, Ellspa. That is not a message *I* would ignore."

"It proves nothing. Also, consider that Blade will need time to work his magic. If we ride now, we may come upon the Uchendi before they are ready for battle. If we wait as you wish, the Uchendi may make themselves too strong even for you and your warriors."

The attempted flattery did not impress Teindo. "Perhaps. And perhaps not. To charge like a bull *shpuga* in the mating season, that is not worthy of the warriors of the Rutari."

"You fear the lawless ones, it seems to me. Has your courage deserted you? Is the only weapon you can still use the one between your—"

He slapped her. Hard, much harder than she'd slapped him. She rocked on her haunches but did not fall over or make any effort to stop him with her mind, although she could probably have done so. She merely glared at him and spoke with anger crackling in her voice.

"Go on. Strike me, beat me, kill me. And then the Rutari will learn of what you did and kill *you*. There will be no one to lead them, the Uchendi will learn of this, and no English magic will be needed to destroy us. Follow your anger where it leads you, Teindo. Follow it and destroy your people."

For those words Teindo wanted to strangle Ellspa slowly. He also knew that she was telling the truth. He was certain that she wanted an immediate war against the Uchendi because she felt betrayed by Blade, not because she'd thought out the wisdom of the matter. He was certain that his own fears of a trap were justified.

He was also certain that he and Ellspa had to agree in the sight of the tribe. The Rutari were in too much danger to permit quarrels among their leaders. Perhaps she would think again if there was bad luck in the war.

And perhaps the River of Life will flow straight up into the sky and water the Gardens of the Moon.

He sighed. "Ellspa, it will be as you wish. I ask only one thing, that we take only riders and *shpugas*. No one on foot. And we take no prisoners. Those Who Went Before must ask for some other offering until we have the Idol safe home again."

"I do not question any of this," said Ellspa. "Forgive me, that I doubted your manhood or wisdom." Her eyes glowed with the anticipation of victory as she came into his arms.

Chapter 25

A Uchendi warrior ran up the hill to where Blade and Eye of Crystal lay side by side behind a rock. He was hardly more than a boy and carried only a spear and a knife. The archers were too valuable to use as messengers. Most of the archers were also older warriors who considered such a task beneath their dignity. Fortunately most of them could shoot well enough to deserve their bows, but Blade couldn't help wondering how many expert archers were being lost by this respect for seniority.

"Winter Owl says that from his place he can see smoke over Red Stones village," said the messenger. "To him it has the look of the Rutari warriors."

That seemed likely enough. "Have any of our people come out of the village?"

"Not yet."

The Rutari burning the village might not be the main body. Until messengers came from the rear guard holding the village, Blade couldn't be sure. Until he was sure, he didn't dare order either Winter Owl with the archers or Friend of Lions with the cavalry into movement.

There were several routes the Rutari could use to advance from Red Stones village. Blade's plan would work only if they used one that let the archers spring an ambush. Otherwise he would have to refuse battle, then keep the Uchendi under control until they could retreat under cover of darkness. Moving five hundred warriors by day would raise a dust cloud a child would recognize.

Also, any further retreat would expose half a dozen more Uchendi villages to the enemy. If they were all evacuated of everyone but the warriors, the Rutari would surely become suspicious. If they weren't evacuated— Blade closed his mind to the thought of what would happen to the women and children. They would have to fight here, if the Rutari gave them half a chance.

"Return to Winter Owl with this message," said Blade. "Tell him to stay where he is until he hears the strength of the Rutari at Red Stones. By then I will have come to him myself." The archers were the key to the battle; Blade wanted them under his personal control. At worst, the cavalry could save themselves by retreating fast, which the archers on foot could not do.

Retreats would do no more than buy time, though, and at a gruesome price. The Uchendi needed a victory.

The smoke of the burning village was growing so thick that Teindo wanted to cough and his *ezinti* was showing signs of distress. He refused to move back as long as his men were plunging even deeper into the smoke to search the huts and houses.

At last they came out. All of them were as black as if they'd been swimming in a tar pit and coughed like old men with rotten lungs. Several were staggering and being helped along by comrades. One was being carried; his arms and legs hung down in a familiar way.

The men carrying the body set it down. "There was an Uchendi in one hut, doomed by a belly wound. So he chose to take one of us with him."

"Any other warriors?"

"No living ones. Three bodies."

"Anyone else?"

Several heads were shaken. "No women, no children,

and not much that could be carried away. A few baskets of dried fish and greenfeet to eat, that was all.''

"Same as the other two villages," someone added.

"Thank you for telling me what I already know," Teindo growled to cover his unease. He turned his mount and rode out of the village as the warriors headed for the well to wash off the soot. At least the Uchendi were not blocking the wells!

Ellspa was sitting cross-legged at the edge of the fields on her leather mat with her women around her when Teindo rode up. He dismounted and told her what he and his men had found. She frowned.

"Three times they do this. They are saving too many of their women and children. Also, the *ezintis* do not feed as they should. They grow weak. I can hear this.''

Teindo looked at her sharply. This was no time for her to enter *kerush-magor* merely to read the thoughts of animals! If she'd learned something more important, however—

But Ellspa looked fully in the waking world. Her eyes met Teindo's straight and clear. "This is not as I expected. I did not think the Uchendi were foolish, but neither did I think they were wise enough to do this once, let alone three times. Perhaps Blade has taught them more in less time than I thought he would need.''

Teindo's joy at this admission was tempered by his suspicion that she was testing him. She wanted him to advise her about what they should do next, in order to see if he would advise caution. He would not fall into that trap. Also, there were the hungry *ezintis* and Great Hunters.

He pointed at the horizon to the south. "There lies the Mountain of the Ice Cave. On either side of it are valleys wide enough to let us all move freely. The nearest other valleys like that are a day's march to the east or two days to the west. Nearer than that are only little trails where we could lose Great Hunters and *ezintis*.''

"What lies beyond the Mountain?''

Definitely he was being tested. She knew that as well as he did. "More villages of the Uchendi than I can count on the fingers of one hand. If we come upon them suddenly, we will have their women and children, certainly their food and houses. Perhaps we can then offer to sell the villager back to the Uchendi in return for the Idol."

"Once we have them, I will listen to that idea again. For now, let us march." She stood up.

Teindo thought of sending a handful of the best riders down each valley to make sure there were no Uchendi in them. However, that would seem cautious. Even worse, by the time the riders came back it would be too late to get the whole of the Rutari through the valleys before nightfall. Then a few Uchendi could do much harm, and surely accidents would take their toll of the beasts.

Also, riders who might give warning of Uchendi could also give warning to Uchendi. Haste could give the Rutari the advantage of the element of surprise. Against a man like Blade they would surely need it.

By the time Blade and Crystal reached Winter Owl, the last of the rear guard from Red Stones village was also coming up.

"It's all of them we expected and more," said the warrior in command. "A hundred *shpugas*. Five hundred warriors. Remounts, the young Wise One, girls for fun at night, everything you'd expect."

"Good," said Crystal briskly. "When they are all dead, the Rutari will not even think of war until the time of our sons' sons."

Blade would personally have said "if" rather than "when," but otherwise she was right. The Rutari were making an all-out effort to take back the Idol. Smash them now, and the ancient war between the two tribes would probably be decided for all time in favor of the Uchendi.

"Best you keep down," said Winter Owl, looking at

Blade and Crystal. "I think there are no Rutari following the men from the village, but if there are they might learn too much by seeing you." He led Blade and Crystal into the cover of some scruffy trees at the bottom of a little gulley.

As much as Blade wanted to be out where he could see, he had to admit that Winter Owl was right. Both he and Crystal were eye-catching. Since each wanted the other to wear the Guardian's full war costume, they'd compromised on both doing so—beads, leather leggings, embroidered headbands, shell-set loinguard, copper bracelets, and all. Blade wore his feather bonnet and had made another for Crystal.

Both were also armed to the teeth—two knives and a spear apiece. Blade carried his plastic bow and a quiver of carefully picked arrows, half poisoned and half plain. Crystal carried the Idol.

Much to Blade's surprise, both the UZI and its ammunition were still useable. He'd fired off half a magazine, then let Crystal dry-fire it.

Blade didn't expect Crystal to find the UZI a very useable weapon. He had her carry it mostly because he hoped that fear of having the Idol recaptured would make her stay clear of the fighting. He wasn't terribly optimistic— Crystal was too fond of a good fight—but it was his only hope.

They sat down in the shade, and Cheeky crawled into Blade's lap. "What do we do now?" asked Crystal. She obviously had at least one suggestion.

"We wait."

"Is that all?"

"You spend nine days out of ten in war waiting. You spend the other day being scared out of your wits."

"You are without fear, Blade."

"No. I'm not *that* big an idiot. I just don't listen to what fear tells me."

The warning system was simple. The Rutari would be

met today only if they came through one of the two passes
around the Mountain of the Ice Cave. A handful of archers
were hiding on top of a cliff that gave a good view of the
entrance to both valleys. Stretching back from the cliff to
Winter Owl's command post were other archers, placed at
two-hundred yard intervals. Each had a red arrow and a
green arrow. A red arrow meant the east valley, a green
one the west valley. When the outpost sent word, each
archer would shoot the appropriate arrow to the next man
down the line. The message would get to Winter Owl and
Blade within minutes.

This was Winter Owl's idea, and Blade was sincere in
praising the chief for it. The Uchendi were clearly people
ready to think for themselves if given a little push. Blade
and recent events had been pushing rather hard.

It was a hot day and neither Blade nor Crystal had got
much sleep the night before. Both had more important
things to do, knowing it might be the last time they'd be
together. Crystal was asleep and Blade was getting
drowsy when they saw Winter Owl hurrying down the hill.

In his hand he held a red arrow.

"So it's the east valley," he said. That was the wider of
the two, and the whole floor of the valley would not be
within bowshot. The archers might have to move into the
open to kill all the *shpugas*, and if they did that many of
them would surely be ridden down or speared. They would
think it was a small price to pay for the life of their people.

"Very well," said Blade, shaking Crystal awake. "Call
in the outposts and messengers, and let's be on our way."

The valley to the east of the mountains was so broad
that Teindo stopped the advance for an hour to move the
Rutari into a new form of marching. When they moved on,
the Great Hunters and their leaders moved in one line close
to the left side of the valley. The *ezinti* riders moved in a
second line down the middle of the valley. A hundred paces
separated the two lines.

"Do you fear an attack after all?" said Ellspa, reining in so close to Teindo that her bare leg pressed against his.

"Hardly. There are hiding places for no more than a score of men within spear-cast. If such a handful did come against us, we would suffer more from our own beasts than from them. Nothing can frighten a Great Hunter." He felt like adding, "They are too stupid," but that was not a lawful thought. "*Ezintis,* however, will take fright if surprised. The Great Hunters will do better work if they do not have frightened *ezintis* running about among them."

"This is so," said Ellspa. Teindo was relieved that she seemed to be not only in a good mood but willing to follow his lead in matters of war. Doubtless this mood would not last, but if it lasted long enough to get the Rutari through the valley and in among the Uchendi villages, that would be more than Teindo had ever won from her before. Perhaps his risking the anger of his wives by bedding Ellspa was going to be worth it after all.

Chapter 26

"They could not have done better for us if we had asked them ourselves," murmured Crystal. The Rutari army was tramping along the valley toward the hillside, which was full of scrubby trees and little ravines that were hiding the archers. The column of *shpugas* would be passing within easy bowshot even for the enthusiastic amateur bowmen of the Uchendi.

"One shot by each archer and all the *shpugas* will be doomed," she said, grinning in savage triumph. "How could Teindo be so stupid?"

"Keep your voice down," said Blade sharply. "Sound carries a long way around here." Crystal looked sulky for a moment but was silent.

"As for Teindo," Blade went on in a whisper, "I don't think he's being stupid at all. He's done what would be a good job of arranging his men and *shpugas* if we didn't have the bows."

"That means he doesn't know about them."

"True. But it doesn't mean that he won't put up a good fight when the battle starts."

Crystal kissed him. "Well, so be it. I would rather be with you in my body, but if we are to be Spirits—"

Blade put a finger to his lips for complete silence. The first of the *shpugas* were passing below now. If the archers could resist the temptation to start shooting at their ancient foes at once, and wait until they could shower the whole line with their arrows . . .

Blade looked down the valley. A clump of small trees was his mark. When the lead *shpuga* passed that one, most of the line would be in range. With better archers he could have hit all the *shpugas* at once, but he had to do the best he could with what he had. It was likely enough that the *shpuga*-handlers would be too surprised to know what to do with the unhurt ones until it was too late.

A hundred yards to go. Seventy, fifty, forty, thirty—

One of the leading *shpugas* lifted its head and growled. Then it started looking from side to side, obviously suspicious of what it smelled but not sure what the smell meant.

Blade cursed under his breath. Either one of the *shpugas* was exceptionally keen-scented and alert, or some of the ambush party had crept too close to the valley floor. It didn't matter. If the attack was to be a surprise, it had to be launched now.

So Blade rose to his feet, nocking an arrow as he did. By the time he was on his feet, the bow was drawn. A moment later, his poisoned arrow was whistling downhill toward the *shpuga* that offered the best target.

Teindo saw the lead Great Hunter stop and appear to scent prey. Whatever was causing this, Teindo knew he had to find out for himself. The guides of the Great Hunters knew their beasts well—they had to or die—but not enough about other things of war.

He was riding toward the side of the valley when another Great Hunter howled, then a second, then two more. Teindo stared at them. Each one had a thin spear no longer than a man's arm sticking into its hide.

At least that was what his eyes told him. Everything else he knew about war told him that his eyes were lying. Such a small spear could never fly straight enough to hit

anything at such a range, let alone drive through the hide
of a Great Hunter.

He was looking around wildly when he saw the Uchendi
warriors rising from behind bushes and stones on the side
of the valley. They were far beyond spear-cast, but each of
them held something that looked like a large spear. A
moment later small spears showered down about the Great
Hunters, hitting several more.

Teindo gathered his wits and reined in his mount. Now
he could see that the "spears" the Uchendi warriors were
holding were actually curved, and that these curved things
hurled the small spears at the Great Hunters.

New spear-throwers. New magic—or perhaps English
war craft?

In either case, *Blade*.

Teindo knew that Blade was behind this, but did not
waste time looking for him. The Great Hunters were all
howling and screaming now, the hurt ones making the
unhurt ones uneasy. All the Great Hunters' cries were
making the *ezintis* jittery.

Teindo tried to control his mount, watch the battle-
field, and shout orders all at once. "Bring the Great Hunters back, back into the valley!" he bellowed. "Now!
Quickly! Riders, gather to me!" The Great Hunters
seemed more angry than hurt, but if the Uchendi charged
now they might actually be able to kill some of the beasts
with regular spears. No men on foot could charge against
ezinti riders in good order, though, and—

A Great Hunter threw back its head and howled in
agony. Its eyes were red pits, and yellow foam dripped
from its mouth. It cried out again, then sank its claws
into its own body, one hand in the chest and the other in
the belly. Blood began to flow through the dark fur.

Then another Great Hunter did the same. A third.
More—Teindo lost count. Again, the howling of the hurt
ones set off the rest. The valley echoed with the mad cries

of the Great Hunters until Teindo felt as if he was in the middle of a raging thunderstorm.

His *ezinti* and many others were prancing frantically, near to bolting. He could still spare some attention from controlling his mount to think of what must be happening and what he should do about it.

Poison.

Poison on the small spears. It didn't matter if they hit a vital spot in the Great Hunters. They would kill it or at least drive it mad no matter where they hit. Probably it was the Rutari's own *klida* seed poison being used against them.

If it was, the Great Hunters were doomed unless they got out of range and out of the valley. They could not be used again in war until some answer was found to the new spear-throwers. That meant no war at all against the Uchendi. That was a hard thought for Teindo; it would be a harder thing still to tell Ellspa. But the choice was not theirs. Blade had made it for them.

Suddenly Teindo's mount went completely out of control. He felt himself losing his seat and flung himself clear to control his fall. He came down unarmed save for his knife, with a Great Hunter only yards away. Its eyes were half shut with yellow ooze, and it did not see him. Instead it saw the *ezinti* and lumbered toward it. The animal reared and galloped off. Teindo saw four of the short spears sticking in it.

The Great Hunter turned back toward him. He got ready to defend himself as well as he could, since to run would be the end of everything.

Then a short spear sank into the Great Hunter's eye, driving deep enough to reach the brain. The beast lived just long enough to claw at the spear, then fell dead. It was so close to Teindo that its blood and other fouler liquids splashed him. He looked down at the body, and saw that the short spear in its eye was longer than the others the Uchendi had used.

He turned away from the body, in time to see Ellspa riding up. She dismounted without speaking to him, and he saw that her eyes held the wide blankness of *kerush-magor*. She was also naked, and Teindo felt a sudden chill at the knowledge of how far the "Wise One" was likely to be willing to go to save today's victory.

It is beyond saving, he wanted to shout.

He also did not want to be the first victim of Ellspa's mind, so he kept silent.

Blade hadn't expected to save Teindo. He'd simply been trying the range of the wooden arrows and hit the attacking Great Hunter. He didn't mind this unexpected bonus. Teindo's staying alive would make the battle harder, but it would make negotiating a peace easier. The few prisoners the Uchendi had taken all said the same thing: Ellspa was fanatically determined to take vengeance on the Uchendi for every grievance she and her people had. Probably nothing short of the total extermination of the Uchendi would satisfy her. That meant the Uchendi might have to fight until the Rutari were exterminated—unless there was some leader among the enemy saner than Ellspa and not afraid of her.

So far, Teindo seemed to be the only one.

A moment after Teindo hobbled away, Blade regretted shooting the arrow that saved him, because other archers now thought it was time to go man-killing and pulled out their wooden shafts. Most of them fell short or went astray; the Uchendi bows simply weren't strong enough to reach any human targets except the *shpuga*-handlers.

"The *shpugas* are the great enemy!" Blade roared loud enough to be heard clear across the valley. "The *shpugas!* I'll shoot down the next man who hits anything but a *shpuga.*" He lent weight to those words by jumping up and nocking a fresh arrow.

Enough of the archers heard Blade to go back to the important work. It took a while, though, and Blade stood in the open, watching until he was sure things were going right. By then Crystal was up beside him, the Idol slung across her back. Of course that meant Cheeky insisted on coming up and joining the fun, too!

In Home Dimension warfare this would have been dangerous. One burst of fire or a single shell could have wiped out the command group. But there were no guns here, and in any case the first part of the battle seemed to be almost over. Dead and dying *shpugas* littered the ground, surrounded by the corpses of handlers and *ezintis* they'd torn to pieces in their dying agonies. Archers who'd shot their quivers empty were stalking the dying.

Out in the valley, the surviving *shpugas* were wandering among the mounted Rutari, disturbing the *ezintis*. One rider sat his mount a little apart, apparently unafraid of either *shpugas* or Uchendi archers. Then the rider urged the mount toward the valley side and Blade recognized Ellspa.

She was nude and had her arms crossed over her breasts. She had to be controlling her mount with her knees alone, or perhaps just her mind. She certainly wore a marvelously serene expression, which suggested her mind was somewhere else.

A moment later Blade knew where Ellspa's mind was— entering his. This happened too fast for him to be aware of what was happening until she inside his mind. After that he found he could not keep from listening to her. He heard her voice as if she'd been murmuring into his ear:

("Blade, come down to me. Come down and find what you have lost. Come down and find happiness you will not find anywhere else. I will give it to you.")

Blade heard Cheeky protesting and felt a paw on his leg. He kicked backward and heard a *yeeep* of pain. Cheeky did not offer him happiness. Ellspa did. He took a step, then a second. He wanted to run, because what he saw ahead was Zoé, nude, riding a white horse along a surf-lashed beach. Her blonde hair flew out behind her in the wind like a flag.

A girl—he thought he remembered the name was Crystal Eyes or something like that—was in his path. She was in Zoé's path too, and she was raising a submachine gun to cut Zoé down. Zoé, his beloved—

Something was in front of his feet, then under them, as if the ground itself was betraying him. He was falling. He twisted frantically in midair, but he was so intent on Zoé that his reflexes were slowed. He crashed down on the hard ground. Now it seemed there was a weight on his chest and another on his legs holding him there.

Something was hammering at his head, too. It sounded like pain but also like the submachine gun. He couldn't see any more, but the jealous Crystal Eyes must be shooting at Zoé. He had to get up and save her, he had to stop Crystal Eyes—

Something heavy and solid smashed down on his head. The pain grew much louder, then everything was silent.

Chapter 27

Blade awoke with the worst headache he'd had since they stopped using the old booth with the electrodes for the transition into Dimension X. He felt as if several gorillas had been pounding on his skull with sledgehammers.

Headache or no headache, he had to know how the battle was going, or at least if he and Cheeky were in danger themselves. He opened his eyes, which was a mistake, then tried to sit up, which was an even bigger one. With some difficulty, he managed not to groan.

However, his movements attracted attention. He heard a familiar *yeeeep*, and something small and feathery hopped onto his lap. Then his pain-blurred vision made out Eye of Crystal standing over him. It even made out the agony of fear on her face. She had to be reassured.

"I'm alive and—ouch—I *think* I'll be all right in a bit."

"Don't try too hard, Blade. The Rutari are beaten, so there is no need for you to do anything. Lie down again and I will bring you water."

Blade drank half the waterskin Crystal gave him in a few gulps, and that took care of most of the pain in his head. By the time the waterskin was empty, he could sit up and look around without wincing.

Crystal was right. The Rutari were scattered all up and down the valley. They seemed to be more concerned with keeping clear of their own *shpugas* or getting away entirely than with fighting anybody. A few of the Uchendi cavalry were already on hand, discouraging the few bold spirits from trying to make any sort of a stand. Sometimes they had to rein in while archers took care of a *shpuga* or two, but that never took long.

Whatever happened to the warriors of the Rutari, this was the last stand for the *shpugas*. The hairy monsters would never decide a battle in this Dimension again.

Downhill from Blade and Crystal, the bodies of both men and *shpugas* seemed to be lying more thickly than elsewhere. Blade looked harder, saw blood around many of them, then looked at Crystal. She looked down at the Idol, blushing and unable to meet his eyes.

"All right, Crystal. I heard the Idol speak. What did you do?"

"I pointed it at the Wise—at Ellspa—like you taught me. She was trying to keep me from using any weapons to save you. She did not think of the Idol as a weapon, so I could use it. The Idol spoke, but it did not silence Ellspa at first. You were going to her, to the *shpugas*."

("Yes," said Cheeky. "Master Blade, you were not the way you should be. So I made you fall. The Mistress Crystal hit you with the Idol so you did not get up.")

Blade felt his head. Yes, there was a lump there now, about the right size to have been made by the butt of the UZI. "And then what happened?" he said dryly.

"The Idol would not speak," said Crystal. "So I put my mind into it, and it did not fight me. I made move the things that were supposed to move, and it spoke again. When it stopped speaking this time, Ellspa was dead. The other Rutari who saw what happened to her were running away."

No wonder, Blade realized. With the Idol itself passing a judgment on their shaman, the Rutari must have thought they were fighting against the gods themselves. And what Crystal had done with her mind . . . The Idol must have malfunctioned, and Crystal made the parts work again.

"You say you made the parts of the Idol move again? Just like you made that last ball move, in the Great Game of *nor*?"

Crystal blushed even harder and could only nod. Blade grinned.

"I've suspected it was you for some time. I suppose you know you did me a good turn there. Without Winter Owl on our side—"

("Master, the Master Winter Owl is coming. If you do not want him to know this, do not talk about it anymore.")

("Thank you, Cheeky.")

The warning was just in time. Winter Owl came leaping up the hill, covered with blood and dust but smiling and as cheerful as a boy. "I have a message from Friend of Lions," he said. "He brings the riders up the valley to finish the work. He says Blade and the archers should not have all the day's glory."

"We won't fight him over his share," said Blade. He stood up and found that his head behaved itself now. Telepathic duels apparently did no permanent injury. But *why* had he been so weak against Ellspa's attack when he'd fought off the much stronger Guardian successfully? Was Ellspa stronger than the Guardian? Or maybe his memories of Zoé would always leave him vulnerable.

That was something to think about, but later. Right now, he had a battle to finish, as long as Teindo might still be alive. He whistled Cheeky up onto one shoulder, slung his bow on the other, and led the way downhill.

The battle faded away rapidly after the mounted Uchendi arrived. The mounted Rutari were no match for the plainsmen, and Blade wasn't surprised at this after he found Teindo's body.

Somehow, with three bullets from the UZI in her body, Ellspa had been able to keep on her feet for a while. Dying, she'd reached Teindo before her strength finally failed her. He would not leave her, even when a dying *shpuga* attacked. He died where he stood, and now man, woman, and beast lay almost on top of each other. Their blood made a wide pool around them, and flies were already beginning to gather. Blade noticed that even Winter Owl did not care to look at the sight very long.

Good. Maybe the Uchendi won't try to exterminate the Rutari after all. And when I take the Idol with me, maybe these people will stop worshiping weapons-magic. Perhaps the idea that there's such a thing as too much killing is about to take root in Latan.

In the face of the Uchendi riders the Rutari either ran or died. Most of them did both. By nightfall the Uchendi were back in Red Stones village. Only a few huts were still habitable, but Blade and Crystal were given one of them.

They lit a fire on the hearth and sat down, too tired to even take off their Guardian regalia. In one corner they piled Ellspa's equipment, which they'd found in the saddlebags of her straying *ezinti*. *Shpuga*-repellant, staff, aphrodisiacs, enough *kerush* seed to put a whole tribe into *kerush-magor*—Ellspa had come well-equipped.

It hadn't done her any good.

Blade leaned back against the wall, realizing how much of the day he'd spent running on sheer willpower. Having that vulnerable spot called "Zoé" reached had taken something out of him that a normal battle didn't. The mere fact of that vulnerability didn't bother him. Indeed, it taught him more about himself and telepathy. That did no harm.

The only problem was—what else might be lurking inside him, ready or at least able to be reached telepathically? "Know yourself" was always a good idea; if you were working with telepathy, it might be a life-or-death matter.

Well, tonight was no time for life-or-death matters. Rather, it was time for living—and for one particular kind of living. Blade reached out an arm for Crystal, and she snuggled into its curve.

She felt so warm and comfortable against Blade that it was a moment before he noticed his head throbbing. Then he sat up, pushing her violently aside.

"Blade, what—?" She sounded concerned rather than angry or frightened.

"Another attack—English magic kind of attack," he said. The pain was mounting and the words came out only with difficulty. He shifted to telepathy.

("Cheeky. We go Home. Get some *kerush* seeds and come to me.")

("Home?" came Cheeky's questioning reply.) But he was already digging in Ellspa's gear. He radiated joy as he found a pouch of seeds, then leaped toward Blade. Blade caught him in his arms and then grabbed the Idol.

("Blade?" cried Crystal. "I don't think this is an attack. You aren't afraid. You're going back to England, with Cheeky?")

Blade couldn't manage a word now even in his mind, but he tried to give her an affirmative. Then the pain ebbed just enough to let him give a clearer message.

("Yes. It is a friend doing the magic, not an enemy as I thought. Stay away from me, Crystal. You might be caught in the magic. Stay here, be happy.")

("I will, I will.") She wanted to cry but was fighting it back.

("Good girl.")

She will do damned well as the first female Guardian of the Uchendi, was Blade's last thought in the Dimension of the warriors of Latan.

Chapter 28

Lord Leighton sat at his desk and contemplated the laboratory reports on Blade's trip to Latan. He also contemplated the complexity of the Universe. At times it seemed as if that complexity altogether exceeded the bounds of reason. This was one of those times.

Leighton knew there was no real reason why the Universe should be so regulated as to be comprehensible to him or to anyone else. He did not really have the right, as a mere human, to feel a sense of personal grievance against those in charge of arranging such matters.

Nonetheless, he did. He also felt more than a little frightened. What Blade had brought back from the last trip was throwing far too many questions about time, space, and Dimension X into the melting pot. Leighton felt as if he were sliding down an ice-coated hillside on a black night with the wind howling about him and strange shapes lurking in the darkness just out of range of clear vision.

He would have felt still worse if it hadn't been for three things.

One was Blade's and Cheeky's safe return. They were now at Blade's country house, supposedly relaxing, but Leighton figured Blade had probably recommenced on the remodeling of the old house already. Blade couldn't sit idle for long.

The second good thing was the gun Blade had brought back from Latan. J's weapon experts had studied the submachine gun and confirmed what the markings indicated: that the UZI was from Englor. That meant that someone else—and someone who was not an enemy—was capable of Dimension X travel. Just how capable they were was something Leighton might not ever learn, but if he did, it might just be possible that England and its inter-Dimensional counterpart—Englor—would be able to pool their knowledge and capabilities.

Leighton picked up the UZI and pulled the trigger. The only sound was an empty click. The weapons experts had said that the gun was beyond repair. But Crystal had fired a round. Had the woman really made the gun function with only her mind?

"Telekinesis . . ." Leighton murmured to himself and shook his head. "Perhaps it can also move a person the way it can move an object. . . ." Well, enough of this speculation, Leighton thought. There would be time to consider telekinesis later.

Now Leighton scanned the laboratory report on the *kerush* seed. This was the third good thing that had resulted from this trip to Dimension X. The report said that the key ingredient of the *kerush* could be synthesized without too much trouble. Not without much expense, however, because the processes were costly, but they were well proven for many years in the pharmaceutical industry.

In a few months they could have enough *kerush* for years of experiments in telepathy. Should they go ahead?

Should rain fall down?

The more difficult question was where to begin. They would need both Blade and Cheeky for these experiments, which would attempt to find others with telepathic capabilities. They would hope to find someone who could link up with Blade and/or Cheeky in such a way that he or she would be able to go to Dimension X also.

Whatever the case, the *kerush* seemed to be the key to

telepathy, and telepathy might still be the key to regular travel into Dimension X.

Leighton activated the terminal on his desk and punched in the call for a readout on certain key items of equipment they'd need to produce the *kerush*, as well as the cost of doing so. He'd want to be briefed with all the vital statistics before he sat down to persuade the Prime Minister to release more money from the Secret Fund.